The Daydreamer Chronicles: Book 3

WHERE DREAMS END

Jethro Punter

Email: jpunterwrites@gmail.com

www.facebook.com/thestairwayofdreams

https://daydreamerchroniclescom.wordpress.com/

ISBN: 9781094926490

V070520

*Dedicated to everyone who still dreams with their eyes
(and their minds) wide open*

PROLOGUE

Isabella Farthing was bored. Really, truly, deeply and mind-numbingly bored. For someone used to a life of adventure, where taking impossible risks, facing terrible storms or overcoming dastardly enemies had become an almost unnoticed part of her daily routine, the last few days had been almost unbearably bland. She had tried to spice up her evening the night before by picking a fight with a group of tough looking Drömer, but to her disappointment they had dealt with her deliberately rude comments with perfect manners, doing nothing more than giving her a couple of rather hurt looks before eventually leaving the Inn's small and crowded bar, their drinks unfinished.

She knew that she really ought to feel guilty, but other than a lingering feeling of tiredness, she didn't really feel much at all. "Still," she reasoned to herself as she clicked her right arm into place, pulling the sleeve of her jacket down as far as she was able, with just the slightly dull brass fingers of her hand showing beneath the cuff, "despite last night's shortcomings perhaps today would be the day that would bring something more interesting, a proper reason to get out of bed."

In truth, she doubted that today would actually offer anything better than any of the repetitively dull and frustrating days from the last week, but there was no harm in hoping. If nothing else there might at least be a chance of better news, some progress made on the repairs to her ship. She rolled her shoulder a couple of times to confirm that her arm was locked securely in place and then shuffled herself around on the thin mattress. Pushing herself forward, she lowered the socket strapped to her left leg onto the smooth brass peg-leg that sat ready and waiting for her at the side of the bed. Then, with a well-practiced twisting motion, she attached it and levered herself onto her feet in a single smooth movement, pausing briefly to steady herself.

Making her way to the other end of the room, which was a matter of no more than five short steps, her room being as small as it was unpleasant, she leant for a moment with her hands resting on the small cracked sink and looked at herself in the mirror. The face within the frame was still familiar, but she increasingly struggled to think of it as her own. She was certain that she must be both younger and happier than the rather tired, middle-aged woman looking back at her from within the cracked, murky glass. With a sigh, she rooted around in the bowl that sat carefully balanced on the shelf directly below the sink, eventually pulling out the small round orb that it contained, despite its best efforts to slip through her fingers which were still clumsy with early morning cobwebs.

Wincing slightly, as she did every time that she pressed the orb into the empty socket that used to hold her left eye, she blinked a couple of times and looked at herself in the mirror again. "Better," she thought, "definitely better." The piercing green of the glass eyeball, whilst in no way a match for the natural hazel of her remaining eye, was a familiar sight and one that made her immediately feel far more like herself.

Her morning routines complete, Isabella clanked and clicked her way back across to the room's door, ducking a little to fit her tall frame through the doorway. Navigating the steep, winding stairway was a tortuous affair, as it was every day, but the small attic room was the cheapest that the Inn had to offer, and she needed to save every thread she could. Every morning when she made her way to the docks it seemed that it was to be informed of ever-increasing repair costs, to the point at which she was beginning to worry that she was going to be land-locked forever. A thought that she couldn't bear to contemplate for more than a moment. As Isabella left the Inn the Innkeeper scowled nervously at her, presumably due to her bad behavior the previous evening. Despite this, as she left the building the morning light was a welcome change from the dank darkness of her room, and momentarily lifted her mood.

In fact, the day proved to be extraordinarily hot, and by the time she reached the docks the brass of her right hand was glowing slightly, drawing even more curious looks than she usually got. Flimsy Jim was waiting for her when she arrived at the yard, pacing nervously up and down, muttering to himself.

"Um...h..hello B..Bella," he stuttered in greeting, looking up for a moment, before dropping his gaze and resuming his pacing.

"Morning Jim, how's my girl doing?" He grimaced at her question, and if anything, the speed of his pacing increased. As Jim had repeatedly informed her despite her complete disinterest, he suffered terribly with his nerves, with both his stutter and his pacing triggered by anxiety. From the look of him this morning he was feeling extremely nervous.

"So?" she asked again, "how are we doing?"

"Uhhm... n...not all th...that good," he managed. "The d...damage to the h...hull was w...w...w...worse than I thought."

Isabella sighed inwardly, trying to keep her temper in check. "How much worse... or more specifically, how much more expensive are we talking?" This conversation was an unpleasantly familiar one, to the point that it had pretty much become part of her daily routine. As a result, Isabella could pretty much predict what the next minute would consist of, unconsciously counting it all out in her head as she watched Jim:

1. 10 seconds of further nervous pacing
2. A sigh as he pulled a piece of paper from the pocket of his overalls

3. 10 more seconds as he studied the paper before scrunching it back up and placing it back in his pocket. (She had never seen what was written on the paper and was increasingly convinced that there was nothing on it)
4. Another sigh, a shake of his head and then....

"300 threads," he said. "Taking materials and labour into account it would cost another 300 threads."

Isabella felt her heart constrict at his words. After the disappointment of the last few days she thought she had become pretty used to receiving bad news, but there was no way she could find that much, not after all the costs she had already incurred. She also noticed, as she did every day, that Jim's stutter seemed remarkably absent when he was talking about money. Without realising how she had got there she found herself face to face with Jim, the material of his overalls bunched tightly in the grip of her metal hand, holding him with his feet dangling several feet off the ground.

"You little scam artist," she growled, red mist washing in from the edge of her vision. "I've had enough of your games."

"No, no, no, it's not like that at all... honestly it's not," Jim squeaked, his legs pedaling uselessly in the air and his hands grasping the solid brass knuckles still holding him aloft. "It's the m...ma...materials you need. You need the very best materials to s...su...survive on the Dwam and the best doesn't come cheap." His eyes widened as Isabella thrust her face close to his.

"I don't have that sort of money," she hissed. "You have already taken nearly everything I have."

"I can ma...maybe manage for 250..." he flinched as Isabella lifted him even higher. "O...okay... 200 threads, but that's the very b...best I can do."

Although Isabella gave him the most menacing glare she was capable of, (which she knew from experience to be pretty intimidating, the empty glow of her glass eye having broken the spirit of many an unlucky soul), it seemed that Flimsy Jim was unwilling to compromise any further, his natural greed slightly outweighing his equally natural cowardice. Despite his precarious dangling, Jim had managed to cross his arms and now just hung there, scowling.

Reluctantly she dropped him to the ground, and ignoring the stream of complaints that followed immediately after, stalked off with her brass hand clenching and unclenching in a constant, angry, cycle. More than anything she wanted to hit something, but the tiny remaining rational part of her brain knew that wouldn't help, other than to make her temporarily feel better. What she really needed was money, a lot of money, at short notice and with no real means of raising any.

As she continued to walk away from the docks her hunched shoulders slowly relaxed and then slumped as the grimness of her situation fully sank in. More than money, she knew deep down that what she really needed was a miracle.

CHAPTER 1

"What we need is a miracle," Adam sighed to Grimble as they sat either side of the long ornate table which still served as the centerpiece to the old Mansion's dining room. He sunk his chin into his hands despondently. "I thought you said that everyone knew where the Nightmares come from."

He was feeling thoroughly fed up and it was difficult not to let his frustrations spill out, even though he knew his friends were only trying to help. When he had found out his mother was still somewhere in the Dream World, and more than that, where she was likely to be, he had been filled with almost unbearable excitement, believing for the first time in what felt like a very long while that he was going to be able to find her. He had been told that she was on the other side of Reverie, in a distant continent across the Dwam, the great sea of dreams, somewhere where the Nightmares that stalked the world came from. But that had been weeks ago, and despite their best efforts, Adam and his odd companions had failed to make any progress.

"That's true," Grimble replied, pulling Adam's attention back to the conversation at hand. "I know, Lucid knows, we all know... but getting there is not so easy."

Lucid nodded in agreement, pushing his chair back away from the table and stretching out his long limbs with a yawn. "The problem is finding a ship that is capable of crossing the Dwam, and more tricky than that, finding a captain that is willing to make the journey." He cracked his knuckles as he finished speaking, a nervous habit which Adam had noticed Lucid had picked up recently and which was emphasised by his unusually long fingers. Adam winced at the sound, rubbing at his own knuckles in sympathy.

"So, what do we do then?"

"Well," Lucid replied, "I have tried pretty much everywhere... and spoken to everyone I can think of in Nocturne..." he paused awkwardly and Adam knew what was coming next. "...everyone except Bombast."

Adam thought back to the last time they had sat together in Bombast's opulent offices at the Grand Library in the centre of Nocturne. Although it had taken a while, he had learned to see through the larger than life pantomime that Bombast portrayed to the rest of the world, past the ridiculous outfits and booming voice. He had glimpsed the shrewd, calculating brain that sat backstage in Bombast's head, hidden away but always working, pulling the levers of Nocturne and beyond. He wasn't sure if there was such a thing as a spymaster in Reverie, but if there was then Bombast was most definitely it.

He knew everything and everyone in the Dream World, and so normally he would have been the first person that they would have gone to for advice or help, especially as, according to Bombast, he had attempted to sail the Dwam himself in his wilder youth. But their relationship with Bombast had been damaged, perhaps irreparably, by the events that had recently taken place in the distant and very unusual city of Moonshine. While they had managed to save the city and deal with the terrible threat it had faced, this had also resulted in the disappearance of Bombast's brother into the mists of the Weave. Although it hadn't been Adam's fault, instead being the result of a clash with some of the other, highly unpleasant, employees of Chimera, he had been present when Bombast's brother had tumbled into the pink mists. Adam also knew that the only reason the clash had taken place was because of him, and so he still felt responsible.

It was an unpleasant feeling that had rested on his shoulders ever since, like a damp, heavy, miserable scarf.

He had gone to visit Bombast, accompanied by Lucid, as soon as they had returned, but Bombast had refused to see them, too consumed by grief at the disappearance of his brother. Lucid had tried several times since then to meet with his old friend... to get the chance to explain what had happened back in Moonshine, but so far without any success. Despite all of this Adam was pretty sure that even now, if Bombast was made aware of the desperate nature of their need, he would somehow see his way to helping them, but he was similarly sure that if there was any way to solve their current predicament without troubling Bombast again then they should take it. The only true solution was to give Bombast time and space, letting his oversized heart recover from its pain, then they could talk, and eventually try and rebuild their friendship.

"It's fine," Adam told him. "I really want to talk to Bombast too, but it's still too soon. We'll have to think of something else."

Grimble leant forward across the table, his heavy-set face resting on steepled fingers. He looked exhausted, the scars on his face seeming more pronounced than normal, the grey of his hair more noticeable. "There is someone else," he said, his deep, gravelly voice sounding as tired as he looked. He turned to look at Lucid. "You could ask Granny."

"Granny?" repeated Adam incredulously, trying without complete success to stifle a laugh. "Who's Granny?"

Lucid looked back across at him grimly. "Not someone you laugh at for a start," he replied, "and not someone that I would choose to speak to... and definitely not to ask for help."

He sighed quietly to himself before continuing, "but Grimble is right, I can't think of anything... or anyone else, no matter how bad an idea it might end up being."

"So, you will go and see her then?" Grimble asked.

"Yes... if I must, I will take Adam with me, but you can stay here," Lucid told him. "My nerves can't take having you two in the same room again. Last time we were lucky to get out in one piece."

"She just needs to learn how to accept a bit of constructive criticism," Grimble harrumphed, although he didn't argue. Instead, he slumped a little lower in his seat, giving off waves of silent disapproval.

"Come on then." Lucid tapped Adam on the shoulder before leading the way out of the Mansion and back into the streets of Nocturne.

The first part of their journey was familiar to Adam, the route down to the docks dotted with the normal mixture of daily traffic, bustling street traders and the occasional wandering dreamer. Stepping aside to let a small girl run past, closely pursued by her Nightmare, (which for some reason on this occasion was an angry looking monkey on a tricycle), Adam asked again exactly where they were headed.

"Today we will be going a little further into the docks than you have been before," Lucid told him. "Until now you have seen... perhaps the better side of the city. But as with most places, there are parts of Nocturne which are less pleasant, and that is where we will find Granny."

Whether it was the effect of Lucid's words or something more palpable, Adam was sure he could feel a change in atmosphere as they passed the more familiar sights, sounds and smells of the dockside bazaar and entered an area he didn't recognize. Following closely behind Lucid, he weaved his way between a series of brick buildings and run-down wooden warehouses, all looming mournfully above them.

It didn't take long for Adam to completely lose his sense of direction as they made their way through the maze of rotten buildings, although Lucid continued to stride confidently ahead, with Adam lagging a few metres behind.

Lucid temporarily disappeared from sight as he walked around a corner just ahead, their route squeezing uncomfortably between several particularly tall pitted brick buildings. As Adam followed him around the corner he stopped short, startled by the odd sight now directly in front of him. Lucid was stood facing the biggest man that Adam had ever seen. Despite Lucid's height, the man stood taller than Lucid and his top hat combined... and was at least five times wider. Gulping to himself Adam walked up to join them.

The hulking figure bent down slightly, bringing its huge face level with Lucid's, although still towering above Adam. "Ullo Mr. Lucid," it rumbled, the voice so deep that Adam swore he could feel it vibrating up through his feet.

"Hello Carter," Lucid replied, smiling up at the massive man currently blocking their way. "How are things with you?"

"Can't complain, Mr. Lucid, Granny keeps me busy."

"And have you been behaving yourself, Carter?" Lucid asked, seeming to be completely at ease despite the less than pleasant surroundings and the fact that the hulking figure he was chatting with had fists much bigger than his head.

"Heh, depends on your definition I s'pose Mr. Lucid. I do what Granny says to do... so you'd best ask her."

Straightening up, Carter stepped slightly to one side, leaving a small gap between him and the nearest wall. One massive hand gestured towards the doorway behind him.

"Through you go then... make sure you behave though Mr. Lucid. I wouldn't want to have to 'urt you," he added, with a pleasant smile as they walked past, Adam pressing himself closer to the wall than he probably needed to, scraping his back against the rough brickwork.

As they entered the doorway the gloom of the alleyway deepened even further, Adam's eyes slowly catching up with rest of his body and adjusting to the darkness.

"Who was that?" Adam asked as they made their way down a dark and rather musty corridor, the walls of which were paneled in a rich dark wood that seemed out of keeping with the otherwise grubby surroundings.

"Carter?" Lucid replied, running his fingers nonchalantly along the paneling. "I've known him since he was little, or at least littler than he is now. He's not a bad fellow at heart, but he is unfortunately rather easily influenced... and for the last few years Granny has been the one doing the influencing." He stopped, flicking the gathered dust from his fingers with a tutting sound. "Sadly, Granny is not the best role model, but she looks after him and keeps him out of trouble... other than the trouble she wants of course."

At the end of the corridor was a surprisingly ornate door, looking like it might be more at home in a Stately Home or a palace than the run-down surroundings of the docks.

"It's not what I expected in here," Adam said, taking in the ornate carving on the door and a very expensive looking portrait hanging just off to one side, showing a haughty man, looking down his nose at the world outside the painting.

"It's an interesting story," Lucid told him, "and one which explains a lot about Granny."

"Do we have time for stories?" Adam asked, although he had to admit he was intrigued, despite his keenness to meet the mysterious 'Granny' and see if she was able to help them.

"I think it's a tale worth hearing before you meet her," Lucid told him, with a sparkle in his eyes that suggested he was as keen to tell the story as Adam was to hear it. "They say that back when Granny was starting out down here in the docks, she crossed paths with the Right Honourable Donald Fitzroy. He is the superior looking chap you

11

might have spotted in the portrait. He had an interest in a number of businesses in this area, and one day when he was visiting he bumped into Granny, although that wasn't the name she went by back then. She was begging on the streets at the time, scraping together the first few threads that started her on her way."

"What was she called then?" Adam asked, "I presume that she still had a name."

"She probably did," Lucid replied, "but nobody knows it now. She is just 'Granny' to friend and enemy alike. No one asks, and I would encourage you to show the same discretion. Anyway... he mocked her in the street, showing off to one of his business associates. They say he kicked over her collection plate, called her a few rude names and then didn't think anything more about it... or her."

Adam raised his eyebrows, "and...?"

"He owned a huge manor house just outside of Nocturne," Lucid continued, with a gesture taking in the surrounding corridor and the opulent decoration. "Years later, when Granny had established herself down in the docks she went after Fitzroy. While he hadn't given her a second thought, I understand that she had thought about him, and that moment back down on the streets, quite a lot. She took him for everything he had. He lost his businesses, one after another, and eventually his home. She stripped everything of value from his Manor House and had it shipped down to the docks, used it to decorate her offices. It serves as a reminder, you don't cross Granny, she doesn't forgive and she doesn't forget... ever."

His story complete, Lucid knocked politely on the heavy wooden door and then stood waiting, head tilted to one side, listening intently. A few minutes passed silently, and when Adam went to step forward, Lucid raised a warning finger to him and mouthed the word 'wait' to him. A further long and increasingly boring minute ticked away and then a small bell, that Adam had failed to see hidden away in a shadowy corner of the ceiling, jangled quietly. Adam jumped slightly, the ringing of the bell bringing back memories from his time in Moonshine that he would rather forget.

Nodding to himself Lucid pushed the heavy wooden door open, which to Adam's secret disappointment didn't creak or make any sort of ominous noise at all.

Despite this rather ordinary entrance, the rest of the room that Adam and Lucid walked into was far more interesting. Although large and well-furnished, the massive amount of clutter made it immediately feel much smaller and slightly cramped. The centre of the room was dominated by a large and intricately carved desk, with a heavy weaved rug directly in front of it. But the rest of the space around this was a chaotic mess of heaped trinkets, ornaments, and other expensive looking knick-knacks. They were piled high on every available surface, with a cluster of fine china vases on the nearest table teetering precariously, squeezed into so little space that Adam was convinced breathing too heavily could cause them to topple and crash to the ground.

Behind the desk was a diminutive old woman, who Adam assumed must be Granny. A face like a slightly rotten apple, wrinkled and brown, stared intently at Adam, the gaze so piercing that he had to look away. When he looked back she had turned her attention away from him and onto Lucid, standing slowly and holding out a hand to him across the desk. Her clothing was faded but expensive looking, a mixture of velvets and lace shrouding her in shapeless, opulent layers.

"So, what do you want from Granny youngster?" Granny asked, her voice a strange mixture of accents that Adam couldn't fully place. The edges of her accent rang with the tuneful melodies of the Sornette's lilting speech, but this was balanced by a much harsher undertone that ran through everything she said, like strands of barbed wire concealed within a harmless looking hedgerow.

"Well... you see we were hoping you could help us find someone..." Adam began, before being interrupted by Granny's rasping laugh.

"Heh... I didn't mean you stripling," she said, "I was talking to your tall friend here." With which she turned her attention back to Lucid, her arm still outstretched.

Lucid lowered his head, planting a kiss on the back of the wrinkled, claw-like hand before straightening up again. Apparently satisfied with this, Granny lowered herself back into her chair with an audible groan of effort.

"So?" she asked him.

"My young companion is correct," Lucid told her. "We are looking for someone, someone with very specific experience. In particular we need a captain, someone who knows their way around the Dwam, someone who has sailed the sea of dreams." He paused as if expecting some sort of reaction from Granny, but she said nothing. Instead, she just sat there looking across at Lucid with a calculating expression on her face.

"You know everything that takes place in the docks," Lucid continued. "Every ship, every trader and every captain that passes through Nocturne. If anyone would know who could undertake a voyage on the Dwam it would be you."

Granny continued to look back at Lucid without speaking, but Adam could see the cogs in her head turning, and after a moment she spoke.

"I presume that this child is the reason you are here?" she asked, pointing to Adam. "An unusual journey for one so young to be undertaking." She turned her attention back to Adam for a moment, beckoning for him to approach with one gnarled finger.

Rather hesitantly Adam walked across to stand in front of her, caught in the glare of the lamps hanging around the desk and the small oasis of clear space that surrounded it. Up close Granny was even more ancient than Adam had first thought and considerably grubbier. The fine clothes didn't appear to have been washed for some time and there was an unpleasant smell that he tried not to react to.

"It's a very rare thing you're asking for," she began. "There are only two captains that I would trust on the Dwam, and unfortunately for you, one of them is quite mad."

"So, who is the other one?" Adam asked. She smiled back at him, not particularly pleasantly, revealing what remained of her teeth. A series of alternating black and brown tombstones in remembrance of long lost and sadly missed oral hygiene. "Oh my..." she giggled, "...you don't understand at all do you? It's the mad one that you need to find. The other one is much, much worse."

"Where then, where do we find this captain?" Adam asked her, trying not to breathe in too heavily, her last exhalation having made him slightly woozy.

At his question she held out a wrinkled hand, the skin on her fingers hanging loose, like oversize jumpers on skinny children, waiting to grow into their clothes. Despite her lack of words, her intention was transparent enough.

"Lucid?" Adam turned to his friend, aware that he had no money of his own. Lucid sighed, gave a shrug and pulled a small velvet bag from his inside pocket. Holding it between the tips of two long, delicate fingers he dropped it into the grasping claw below.

Without even stopping to check the content of the bag, the hand snapped closed and the bag was stashed below the table. "That will do," she said, "as a down-payment. I will be sure to be in touch when it's time for you to... fully repay me for this favour."

Adam looked across at Lucid, there was still a smile on his face, but to Adam it looked slightly more brittle than it had before and perhaps there was even a spark of anger in his eyes for a split second. Then he managed to control whatever momentary emotion had reared its head and his expression returned to one of bland indifference.

"Your lanky Sornette friend will know where she is," Granny continued, a smile returning to her thin blue lips. "There is a great gathering of his people just over a day's travel from here, a Grand Assembly... you will find her there."

"How do you know?" Lucid said, his expression remaining carefully neutral, the only sign of his doubt being a slightly raised eyebrow. "How do you know that she's at the Assembly?"

"She is desperate for money," she replied, still smiling her unpleasantly toothy smile. "I have heard from my various... contacts at the docks that she is out of funds and her ship is still in for repair. She has been banned from every bank, money lender and gaming house in the city, but there is always a game to be played and prizes to be won at the Grand Assembly... isn't that right?" The last comment was aimed at Lucid, who nodded slightly before remembering himself and pausing rather awkwardly mid-nod.

"So what's her name?" Adam asked, regretting speaking as soon as the words left his lips and Granny's grimly smiling attention turned back to him.

"No need to bandy names around stripling," she said, "but she is familiar enough to those that need to know, and she is to all accounts... distinctive."

"Thank you for your time," Lucid said, tapping Adam on the shoulder, giving him notice that their audience was at an end. He nodded again, almost deeply enough to class as a bow, in the direction of the wizened old woman and then pulled open the door, ushering Adam out with him.

As the door closed slowly behind them Adam saw Lucid release a deep exhalation and with it he seemed to deflate slightly. The confident façade from the meeting with Granny leaving him along with his breath.

"See you later Mr. Lucid," rumbled Carter as they ducked past his huge frame on the way back out into the docks. "Look after yerself."

"I will Carter, you take care too," Lucid replied. Then he grasped Adam's elbow, leading him away and trying to stop him from so obviously gawping. As they weaved their way back through the maze of old warehouses. Lucid was walking faster than normal, with an unfamiliar tightness in his movements, like an overwound clockwork toy, meaning that Adam was forced into an awkward half-run to keep up.

Carter watched them go, intrigued by the curious pairing. He couldn't work out why Lucid would be wandering around the docks with a human. A small, scrawny one at that. Then he shrugged to himself, working things out was something he generally left to Granny. He was so caught up in his thoughts that he didn't notice the patch of dark shadow growing slowly on the wall behind him. It started out as small and innocuous as a single oily raindrop, slowly growing till it was a big as a plate, then again until it was nearly as big as Carter himself.

It was only when it was so big that it nearly filled the wall behind him that Carter become aware of it, an uncomfortable warning sensation itching at the back of his head, and by then it was much, much too late.

CHAPTER 2

"What's wrong?" Adam asked as he tried his best to keep pace with Lucid's rapid stride, "we got what we wanted... didn't we?"

"We did," Lucid replied, "and now I owe Granny a favour." He paused mid-stride and turned to face Adam, who reeled back with surprise at the anger on Lucid's face.

"I don't understand..." Adam began awkwardly, still thrown by the unfamiliar fury he could see within his friend.

"You wouldn't... you shouldn't have to understand," Lucid told him, his expression softening slightly. "Owing Granny is something that I promised myself I would never do again." He drew a deep, steadying breath. "When I first came to this city I was a little... naïve and I found myself facing unfamiliar problems. Granny helped me, or so I thought. In return she didn't immediately ask for anything, just told me that I owed her a favour. For years she held that over me, never quite letting me forget." He scowled, the memory obviously an unpleasant one.

"Then one day something happened, something big enough that even Granny couldn't deny that I had re-paid her in full... with interest even... and that should have been it. But now I owe her a favour once again."

"I'm really sorry," Adam said. "We only went there because of me. Because I wanted... needed to cross the sea."

Lucid looked down at him and settled a long-fingered hand reassuringly on his shoulder. "It's not your fault, it's mine. I should have known that you never get anything from Granny without paying the full price. I put too much faith in the value of my previous service, convincing myself that I perhaps maintained a little credit with her, but it appears I was wrong."

Turning back towards the clearer air of the docks, Lucid began to walk again, although at a more measured pace, in consideration for Adam's shorter stride.

"You saw her office, all those precious little items piled high. Every single thing in that room has come from someone that owes Granny. Each one is a record of a favour that she is owed, a down-payment. She likes collecting favours, but she hates to call them in. They are much more valuable to her when they are constantly held over their owner's heads, never knowing when she might want them to do something for her."

"There were so many, all piled up in her office," said Adam, "she must be owed favours by everyone in the city."

"Heh... nearly everyone," replied Lucid, a little of his natural humour returning. "Not Grimble though. He met her once and... they didn't get on... they didn't get on at all."

Surprisingly this memory seemed to lift Lucid's spirits a little, putting a slight spring back in his step. As they left the murky shadows of the high brick alleyways behind them, he tilted his top hat to a jauntier angle, cracked his knuckles noisily and then brushed a speck of dust from his shoulder with a cheerful whistle.

"Come on then Adam," he said. "The Grand Assembly is waiting," his smile broadening into something approaching genuine happiness, "and I can't wait to tell Grimble."

Lucid's smile stayed in place all the way back to the Mansion, although his newly rediscovered cheerfulness definitely didn't rub off on Grimble when they broke the news to him.

"Ugh," Grimble looked at Adam and Lucid with a face even more miserable than normal. "I suppose I have to go with you."

"Afraid so," Lucid replied, without even a vague attempt at making his apology sound sincere. "I could just take Adam, but I think on this occasion there is some benefit in having strength in numbers."

"Fine," Grimble growled, "I am sure that we will all have a wonderful time. If you will excuse me, I think that I need to start packing." Continuing to grumble to himself Grimble stomped out of the room, although Adam could tell that Lucid wasn't at all bothered by his friend's grumpy reaction. If anything, he seemed even more cheerful than he had been earlier, his face almost split in two by a broad grin.

"We will start our journey tomorrow morning at first light," Lucid said, "until then I would suggest you return home and get some rest. It promises to be a busy day."

Although he didn't feel particularly tired, Adam could see the sense in Lucid's words. He could remember the excitement and underlying yearning in Lucid's voice when he had previously spoken of the Grand Assemblies, the great gatherings of the Sornette. If it was anything like the smaller Assembly that he and his friends had visited back when Adam was still new to the Dream World, then it promised to be quite an experience.

When Adam awoke in his bed back in the Henson's house, the prospect of spending his day at school was harder to face than normal. He finally felt that he was making genuine progress in the search for his mother, and although he knew there was nothing he could really do until he returned to Reverie that evening, it was difficult not to wish the day away.

His concentration was even more fractured than normal, with visions of what the Grand Assembly might be like intruding whenever he tried to manage even the simplest of his maths revision questions. Despite this, for once he somehow managed to avoid earning a detention, mainly as Miss. Grudge had been replaced for the day by a cover teacher who was content to let them work through their books in relative silence. Apparently, Miss. Grudge was on a training course, or at least that was what Charlie told Adam as they sat eating their lunch.

"Do you think she has been sent to learn what a sense of humour is?" Adam said, half-way through his sandwiches, stopping to wipe away a couple of stray crumbs.

"Fat chance," Charlie replied. "I reckon she's off to learn new types of detentions, now that she has used up all the normal ones on you."

"Oh ha, ha, very funny."

"So, what's the latest in Reverie?" Charlie looked quickly from side to side as he spoke, but he and Adam were seated well away from the next table, out of ear-shot of their classmates. "Have you managed to find a way to cross the sea yet?"

"Maybe," Adam said cautiously, not wanting to get too carried away. "We have a pretty decent lead to follow. When I go back tonight, we are going to see if we can find a ship and a captain willing to take us."

Charlie's eyes widened. "Sounds a bit dangerous... although I still wish I could go with you."

Adam gave his friend a sympathetic smile. Despite Charlie's one and only experience in Reverie, which luckily he didn't remember, as it hadn't ended at all well for him, he was still desperate to join Adam in what he viewed as a world full of amazing adventures. Adam had tried to explain that a lot of what had gone on in the Dream World hadn't been anywhere near as much fun as Charlie seemed to think, with moments of sheer terror that he would never be able to completely explain, but his friend had an amazing ability to filter those moments out. In Charlie's mind Adam spent his time flying around Reverie like a superhero, and no matter how hard he tried to deny it, Adam couldn't change his friend's mind.

"I know mate... and if there was any way you could go with me you would be welcome. But even Nora doesn't seem able to get back into the Dream World."

This raised a very awkward subject that Adam had been trying to ignore, his concentration already being spread pretty thin by the problems in Reverie. Nora Penworthy, the girl who he had rescued from the Horror back when he had first discovered the Dream World, had more than repaid the favour recently, helping Adam and his companions with all the troubles in Moonshine. Without Nora, and the surprisingly friendly nightmare creature Mittens, he knew it was unlikely that they would have survived their adventure, let alone saved the city.

It had been nice to have someone else who understood exactly what it was like to go to Reverie each night, who had walked the streets of the cities and chatted with Lucid and Grimble. For one thing, it had reassured Adam that he wasn't going mad and that the Dream World was every bit as real as he believed it to be, and for another Nora had been an invaluable companion.

When Mittens, the friendly Incubo, (as far as it was possible for such things to be friendly), had left them after their time in Moonshine, Nora had been worried that her ability to enter Reverie at night would depart along with her. Sadly, and despite Mittens final re-assuring words that, "some doors when opened are hard to shut again," her fears had proved to be very real and Nora had failed to find her way back ever since.

To start off with it had just been seen as a temporary setback with Adam asking Lucid and Grimble for their advice, sure that they would find a solution, but despite their initial optimism nothing had seemed to help. Soon Nora had become so frustrated that she found it almost impossible to speak to Adam and hear about the adventures that she was now missing.

Things had got slowly but increasingly chilly between them and Nora had started to isolate herself, too upset by her inability to help to hear any more about Reverie. Although he still felt bad for her, Adam thought it was completely unfair that she was taking her frustrations out on him.

Today Nora had chosen to sit about as far away from them as it was possible to be without actually sitting outside the hall at lunch-time, and was pointedly looking away every time Adam sneaked a look in her direction.

"Leave her to it," Charlie said, spotting his friend's distracted gaze. "Either things will work out or they won't, but staring across at her all the time isn't going to help."

"I wasn't staring," Adam replied shortly, blushing slightly. "It's just a pity that she won't talk to me anymore."

"I don't see what she's making such a fuss about anyway," Charlie added. "At least she got to go into the Dream World for a while. She should spare a thought for me, I haven't got to go there at all."

Although he still managed to keep his face fixed in a smile, inside Adam gave a deep sigh. Fighting off nightmare creatures and saving the world was starting to feel a lot more straightforward than managing to keep his school friends happy. The only difference was in this world he didn't have any special powers to help him out... and he was pretty sure he was failing.

That night, when Adam finally fell asleep, clasping his mother's pendant tightly where it lay under his pillow, he decided that he was going to concentrate on finding his mum. There were only so many things he could try and deal with at once. His friends would just have to work things out themselves, without Daydreams, or magic, or whatever it was that he seemed to be able to do in Reverie.

That feeling stayed with him as he felt his consciousness pinwheeling through the air as he entered Reverie, looking out for the familiar shapes of Lucid and Grimble's thoughts. Within a few seconds he had spotted them, the spiky bramble of Grimble's brain next to the calmer, rippling sphere of Lucid's. A couple more seconds and he reached them, and with a final effort blinked his eyes open into wakefulness, lying on his back, flat on the deck of Lucid's barge, "The Dreamskipper."

"Welcome back," Lucid greeted him as Adam slowly got to his feet, his eyes adjusting to the light reflecting off the gently rolling mists of the Weave. "We have made good progress since you were last here and are well on our way to the spot where the Grand Assembly is gathering. So long as we continue at our present rate, we should reach it by the evening. And that to be honest, is when the place will just be starting to really come alive."

"Great," muttered Grimble with far less enthusiasm. "A night stuck with a load of partying idiots, searching for an even bigger idiot to help us do something that is so unbelievably idiotic that no one else would even imagine trying it. I am starting to think I might be getting too old for this nonsense." He shuffled off towards the far end of the deck, although every now and then Adam could still hear the occasional further variation on the general theme of "idiots," amongst the grumbling.

Despite Grimble's misgivings, the remainder of the journey passed uneventfully, the weather remaining pleasant, with just enough of a breeze to allow Lucid to use the Dreamskipper's small sail. The sun shone bright and clear, and Adam spent much of the day enjoying the chance to genuinely relax for the first time in a long while, lying back on a makeshift hammock and letting his mind meander (which was like letting your mind wander, but even more aimlessly).

It was just as the sun had dropped down below the horizon and the shade of the evening was drawing in that they rounded a particularly long bend in the Weave and got their first sight of the Grand Assembly. The light from a thousand lanterns spread wide across the far shore sparkled back at them like a reflection of the scattered stars above. From a distance, Adam would have sworn that they were approaching another city, every bit as big and vibrant as Nocturne or Moonshine. However, as they drew closer the reality of the sight in front of them became clearer, the individual shapes of the closely tethered barges gradually emerging from the shadows of the rapidly advancing dusk.

Even taking into account the urgency of their visit Adam could sense that Lucid was especially excited to be getting close to the Grand Assembly. He hadn't said anything, but the nearer they had got to their destination the quieter he had become, staring ahead with something close to longing in his eyes. Adam could still remember the affection in Lucid's voice when he'd previously spoken of the great gatherings of his people, and the tinge of sadness when admitting what he'd given up when he had permanently moved to the city to join the ranks of 'The Five', as one of Reverie's small band of protectors.

"So, what can we expect when we get there?" Adam asked.

"It's the greatest annual gathering of my people," Lucid told him, still buzzing with enthusiasm about their destination. "So, there will be dancing and singing, incredible drinks, delicious food..."

"...and criminals and scallywags, rich idiots and smart con-artists, all squeezed into one giant, floating barrel," Grimble concluded for him with a shudder, "oh and did I mention the idiots..."

Caught between their two, very contrasting views, Adam watched the edge of the temporary floating city drawing closer and closer, not at all sure what they were about to walk into. Presumably they were going to be met by a group of happily singing and dancing Sornette, who would offer them a delicious lunch before robbing them all.

CHAPTER 3

'Souris' Lankin was as small and fast as his adopted name would suggest. For one of the Sornette he was surprisingly short, a result of an upbringing where decent meals were few and far between. Other than his size there was little memorable about him, other than an overwhelming impression of a nervous animal about to bolt.

His size, speed and nondescript appearance had all turned out to be advantages in his eventual choice of career, although choice was perhaps too strong a word when you took into account the series of unpleasant 'guardians' and other shady characters that had led (and sometimes pushed) him down the road that had resulted in his current life of petty crime.

The Grand Assembly had attracted more than its fair share of crooks and swindlers, all keen to secure their slice of the gigantic pie, filled crust to crust with profit, that the gathering represented. Souris' crew had arrived two days earlier and quickly settled on one of the outer neighbourhoods of the Assembly, close to one of the docking areas. While the boss of the crew, a particularly smooth Sornette card sharp and con-man that went by the name of 'Twister' had made his way towards the centre of the city of barges, where the big money was to be made, Souris and several other more junior members had been left on the outskirts.

While it meant they weren't close to the richer pickings found on the biggest barges, they did get first dibs on new arrivals, and it was one of these groups of newly docked visitors that had grabbed Souris' attention.

They were an odd-looking group. A lanky, smiling Sornette, a grizzled Drömer with a constant scowl fixed on his face, and between them a boy who looked no older than Souris himself. To begin with Souris hadn't seen anything particularly special about the group other the rather strange combination of characters, but something had made him decide to follow them for a few minutes all the same. Leaving the regular spot he had picked out for himself the day they had arrived at the Assembly, a shady gap between two makeshift shacks which was too small and cramped for most but just about comfortable for him, Souris made his way across the deck, trailing a short distance behind the group.

It was as the new arrivals crossed the temporary bridge between the outer ring of barges and the rest of the Grand Assembly that Souris spotted the boy's hand resting for a moment on a spot high on his shirt. Looking more closely he saw a slight bump in the fabric of the shirt just below the boy's collar and the glint of a chain hanging around his neck. It wasn't much, but Souris prided himself on his instincts, and there was something about this group and the glint of the concealed pendant that caught his interest.

As he walked Souris flexed his small, slim fingers and began to hum to himself under his breath. He had a feeling that today was going to be a good day.

"This is amazing!" Adam said, unable to contain his enthusiasm. "I thought that the last gathering we went to was pretty fantastic, but this..." he paused, looking around the mass of barges, spreading off into the distance. They stretched out as far as the eye could see, and in the case of the Sornette, with their lively chatter, bartering and arguing, laughing and singing, also as far as the ear could hear. "This is something else...."

Lucid just nodded, obviously pleased by Adam's reaction, his own excitement at being back amongst his people shining in his eyes,

27

although it seemed to Adam that there was still an unexplained and underlying tinge of sadness behind it all.

"It's a rare occasion when such a gathering comes together," he said after a moment, "and this must be one of the biggest that I have ever seen. Sornette from all over the Great Dream are here, and for a few days at least we can show the rest of Reverie how to have a good time.

"So, it's just a big party then?"

"No... although there is certainly an air of celebration," Lucid told him. "It's much more. Many important trading agreements will be made during the Assembly. Treaties, and deals between the various clans will be put in place, and when there is a change in leadership then the new Mamans will be confirmed."

"It's also the biggest collection of miscreants, dodgy dealers and general skulduggery you will ever be unlucky enough to find," Grimble broke in, his voice laced with disapproval. "The Sornette are flighty at the best of times, a magnet for all sorts of bother, and when you get a big group like this... well, you need to watch yourself and your pockets. You know what they say...."

Although he felt he shouldn't encourage Grimble any further, not least because his grouchiness seemed to be taking the edge off Lucid's good mood, Adam couldn't stop himself from asking, "No I don't... what do they say?"

"If a Sornette shakes your hand, then make sure to count your fingers afterward," Grimble gave Lucid a sideways glance, a grim smile playing around the corners of his mouth.

Lucid just smiled back at this. "Keep your hands in your pockets then... come on Adam, let's go," and he set out again, striding across the deck of the nearest barge. Adam followed shortly behind him, eyes wide, taking in the varied sights. Directly ahead of them a couple of Sornette traders were haggling enthusiastically with a Drömer woman who seemed singularly unimpressed with whatever it was they were offering, her arms crossed and her expression determinedly grim. Behind the two Sornette there was a large cage, hanging from an ornate stand. It contained a bird with gloriously bright plumage that shimmered in the lights of the barge, each feather sparkling like the edges of a sharply cut gem. Every now and then one of the Sornette would gesture back behind them, pointing to the bird and then waving their hands excitedly, none of which seemed to have any effect on their reluctant customer.

Fascinated by the scene Adam was disturbed for a moment by a particularly small and skinny Sornette who, apparently also distracted by his surroundings, bumped into Adam and knocked him slightly to one side, before walking off with a muttered apology.

"No problem," Adam replied automatically, regaining his footing and following after Lucid, who had set off again towards the centre of the gathered barges.

A couple of minutes later they had reached their destination, a large vessel that looked like it was being used as a central marketplace for the gathered Assembly. A variety of stalls and stands were spread across the large, flat deck and the shouts of various traders, entrepreneurs, and chancers floated through the air, creating a tapestry of noise that Adam found intoxicating.

Adam's attention was immediately drawn to one of the food-stands, fairly close to where they were standing. The stallholder was a young-looking Drömer, her facial hair a light brown, with braids to either side, threaded through with beads, giving her an individual, bohemian look a world apart from Grimble's dour appearance.

She was serving up some sort of stew or thick soup, ladling the steaming liquid into large wooden cups, which her customers were eagerly digging into with the help of chunks of roughly cut bread. Adam wasn't sure what was in the soup, but even from this distance it smelt amazing, and his stomach gave him a quick rumbling reminder that he hadn't eaten for quite some time.

Reaching into his pocket Adam rummaged around for one of the coins that Lucid had given him back on the Dreamskipper, but after a minute of searching first one pocket, then the other, he had only found a tissue, some nondescript fluff and a complete absence of coins.

"Lucid?" Adam called across to his friend, "have you got a spare couple of threads I could use please?"

"What happened to the coins I gave you?" Lucid asked, "you haven't spent them already?"

"No... I must have dropped them I suppose, sorry," Adam patted himself down one final time, and as he did his blood ran cold. Where the familiar touch of his mother's pendant normally lay against his chest there was... nothing. The deck of the barge felt like it was swaying under his feet and his vision blurred queasily.

The next thing he knew he was looking up at Lucid's concerned gaze. "What's wrong Adam?" his friend asked, "one minute you were fine and the next you're flat on your back."

"My pendant," Adam managed, unable to find the words for the sudden horror he felt. His stomach felt cold and empty, like he was about to throw up, and his arms and legs were still failing to do what he wanted, waves of shivering nausea running up and down them. "My pendant has gone..."

Lucid's eyes narrowed and he crouched down to bring his face level with Adam's, gripping his shoulder with long fingers. "I should have kept a closer eye on you," he said. "Try and think back, anything odd or unusual..."

It was hard to do anything other than let his mind spiral down into an unthinking panic, like water down a plughole, but Adam tried his best to concentrate. He couldn't really think of anything, with his brain refusing to concentrate on anything other than the horrifying thought that the pendant was gone. Then out of the corner of his eye he saw the small, darting figure of a young Sornette crossing the connecting walkway at the far end of the barge and he remembered his bump from earlier.

"I got bumped into earlier," he said, desperately trying to think back, "... and I am pretty sure that it was that boy over there." He pointed to the back of the little Sornette who had now crossed to the next barge.

Lucid reached down and grasped Adam's hand, pulling him to his feet. "Come on then," he said, "if it was something to do with him then we can't risk losing sight. We are remarkably lucky to have spotted him now. If he disappears into the crowds at the centre of the Assembly I doubt we would be able to find him again easily."

His legs still felt like jelly, but with Lucid leading the way, Adam followed the rapidly departing figure as fast as he could, with Grimble lagging just behind them both.

CHAPTER 4

They had been tailing the suspected thief for several minutes, slowly gaining ground despite a couple of heart-stopping moments when he had momentarily vanished from sight, only to re-appear from amongst the crowds. The skinny little Sornette scampered across one final walkway and made his way towards a table set in a secluded far corner of a particularly large barge. It was sheltered and shaded under an overhanging awning of bright cloth, flashes of the colour picked out for flickering moments in the lamplight. Although Adam couldn't see clearly from this distance, the Sornette boy appeared to be having a brief whispered conversation with one of the shadowy figures sat at the table.

Compared to the rest of the barges that Adam had crossed, this one had a far heavier and more serious atmosphere. There was no music, no laughter, and very little conversation. Instead all of the attention focused intently on the table, sucking the atmosphere from the rest of the barge.

As they drew closer the individual figures sat around the table become clearer, details emerging from the shadows. Closest to them was a small Drömer woman, hunched protectively over a small cluster of cards held close to her chest. Every now and then she would dart a suspicious, angry look to either side as if daring the other players to try and sneak a peek at her hand.

To her left was a sharp but rather shady looking Sornette, his top hat shiny and new, with a cluster of playing cards stuck into the thick silk band rather than the variety of random knick-knacks that Adam would normally expect to see. His cards were held casually in one long-fingered hand, not seeming to be of any particular importance or interest to him. This initial impression wasn't however borne out by the large pile of shiny treasures stacked in front of him, and there right in the centre of the pile was Adam's pendant, its dull shimmer more or less visible amongst the shinier winnings.

"Look," he hissed to Lucid. "My pendant... that little thief gave him my pendant. We have to get it back." As he spoke the seated Sornette player reached across and ran his fingers across the pendant, before picking it up by the chain and dangling it loosely, giving it a rather bored stare as he did. The sight was too much for Adam to bear and he started to walk towards the table, fists clenched. He was halfway there, angry accusations already forming on his lips, when a hand gripped him by the elbow, halting his progress.

"I know you're angry," Grimble muttered under his breath, trying not to draw the attention of the players or the wider audience gathered around the game, "but we need to be careful, play this sensibly. There are some serious people here."

"And by serious you mean...?"

"I mean that some of them are not very nice," Grimble replied.

"He's right," said Lucid. "For the minute I am afraid that we just watch... and we wait for the right moment to make our move."

And so that's what they did. For the next half an hour Adam spent his time watching each of the players, concentrating most of his attention on the lanky, relaxed Sornette who was enjoying an almost supernatural run of luck. It was unbearable, to be so close to his pendant but unable to claim it. However, despite his growing frustration, Adam had learned to trust his friend's judgement and somehow managed to contain his anger.

Although Adam had never managed to really master it, he had seen Dreamer's Gambit played enough times to understand what was going on. Essentially a very simple game, each of the players would play one of the four suites of cards, either one higher or one lower than the preceding card. Then, once there was a run of 5 or more cards on the table, you could play a matching card and win the pile.

It was so extraordinarily simple to play, not much more than a slightly more complex game of 'Snap' that Adam couldn't understand how he always lost so badly, but he always did. Lucid in particular had a knack of pulling out a matching card just before Adam was ready to play his. Even worse were the times when he was convinced that he was about the win the hand, and then Lucid would pull the Gambit card from the deck, which instantly ended the game.

Watching the game unfolding in front of them, the fancily dressed Sornette seemed even luckier than Lucid. Time after time he nonchalantly laid down the winning card, and one after another the seats around the table emptied as the other players gave up or ran out of treasures to use as their stake in the game. First to leave the table was a large and expensively dressed man with an extravagantly waxed moustache. Smiling broadly at the surrounding crowd he slowly pushed his chair back, brushed some imaginary flecks of dust from his trousers and wandered off with the relaxed smile still on his face. As he passed Adam it looked like the smile hadn't reached as far as his eyes, which held the haunted look of someone who had just lost a lot more than they could afford. It might have been Adam's imagination, but he was fairly sure that a few moments later he heard a muted wail of despair from the spot in the darkness where the man had left the barge.

Next to go was the Drömer woman, who left the table with far less grace, slamming the remainder of her cards down and then stomping off with such ferocity that Adam could feel the planks flexing slightly under his feet as she passed.

This left just two players at the table. On one side was the relaxed-looking Sornette, who now had most of the game's winnings piled in front of him, and almost directly opposite him was his one remaining opponent. She had been partially hidden from Adam's view by the other players, but now they had left he could see her more clearly.

She looked like she was human, although very tall and slim, to the point Adam had initially thought her another of the Sornette. She was wearing a long, dark trench-coat, with a matching tri-cornered hat, long red hair spilling out from underneath its brim. Her expression was grim, her hand clutching her cards close to her chest and her other arm resting on the table, fingers drumming out a nervy beat next to the tiny pile of remaining winnings in front of her.

It was the tapping fingers that caught Adam's attention. The glimmer of the lamps was reflecting off what he had initially taken to be a heavily gloved hand. Now he could see that, rather than a glove, the light was glinting off the joints of long metal fingers, hinged at the knuckles, with slim pistons powering the incessant tapping that had first drawn his attention.

"He's very good isn't he," said Adam, gesturing to the lounging Sornette.

"Hmmm," Lucid muttered back, sounding unconvinced. "He's certainly good, but I'm not sure that his skill at Dreamer's Gambit is what's got him this far.

"What do you mean?"

"I've been watching him during the last few hands," Lucid replied, eyes narrow. "Every time it looks like one of the other players is about to get onto a winning streak, he pulls out the gambit card and ends their run."

"You do that when I play you".

"True, sometimes I do," Lucid admitted, "but you are not, with respect, an experienced player. The others around that table are all good players, much better than me."

"And?"

"And you learn the flow of the cards, when to expect certain cards coming up. You learn when to push for a higher score and when it is best to settle for what you have. Most of all you learn to feel when the gambit card is due to come out... and it has been coming out much more regularly than I would expect... and far, far too conveniently."

"You think he's cheating?" Adam asked.

"I know he's cheating... I just don't know how," Lucid admitted.

Adam looked back at the pile of mixed treasures heaped on the table, his pedant looking rather dull and flat compared to some of the shinier trinkets, but far more valuable to Adam than any amount of money or jewellery could ever be. He had to get it back, but without it he wasn't sure he could manage even a small Daydream, and without his Daydreaming he had no idea how he could get the pendant back.

35

He was still puzzling about what to do next, when his concentration was disturbed by a very unexpected sight. There, walking towards the table and the two remaining players was a figure that he knew extremely well, but which was at the same time completely unrecognisable.

The Drőmer strolling casually towards the table looked like Grimble, with the same grey hair, the same deep scars, but Adam had never seen Grimble stroll anywhere. He wasn't even sure that Grimble was capable of strolling. Normally he walked heavily, like someone permanently angry at the rest of the world and making his feelings known one stamping step at a time. Nor had he had ever seen him wave cheerfully, as he was now doing towards the tall Sornette player, who from the look on his face was just as confused by this sudden interruption as Adam.

"Monty…" Grimble drawled, in a voice that was definitely coming from Grimble's mouth, yet sounded nothing like the deep, rumbling, grumble that Adam was used to hearing, "…you old scallywag, lovely to see you again." By now Grimble had managed to clear a route through the spectators crowded around the table and had nearly reached the players.

"What's he doing?" Adam whispered across to Lucid, who was watching the scene open-mouthed.

"I think he has worked out how that chap is cheating," Lucid replied, as he managed to find his voice again, although his eyes stayed locked firmly on the events unfolding in front of them, "and I presume this is his idea of a plan…"

Grimble, or his identical, incredibly confident and cheerfully upper-class twin, had now reached the Sornette and grabbed his hand, which he was shaking enthusiastically. With his other hand Grimble had grasped the Sornette's arm, gripping it tightly. Taking advantage of the commotion, Adam and Lucid managed to shoulder their way closer to the table and the unfolding drama.

"I'm sorry…" the Sornette was saying to Grimble, somehow managing to sound calm and well-mannered despite the annoyance that Adam could sense bubbling away just under the smooth exterior, "...but I think you have mistaken me for somebody else."

"Don't play games with me you rascal," Grimble replied, apparently unperturbed. "I was asking around everywhere for my good mate back from those happy days at Nocturne University, and when they told me that Monty Stickleback was playing a friendly game of cards on this very barge I just had to dash straight over. So glad I got the chance to catch up with you. It must be, what... fifteen, no twenty, years since we last saw each other." His eyes were twinkling as he spoke, although Adam was fairly sure that the sparkle was a result of Grimble enjoying the mischief he was causing rather than the friendliness it was supposed to convey.

"I am not this... Monty Stickleback you speak of," the Sornette hissed, his cultured front slipping momentarily, his voice increasing in volume as he spoke. "I am Silas Twister, the greatest card player in Nocturne and you are disturbing my game, so if you could please... owww... oouchhh..." His protestations turned into a pained whimper as Grimble gave his arm a particularly strong squeeze and Adam was pretty sure he heard a mechanical twanging sound from somewhere up Twister's sleeve.

"My sincerest apologies," Grimble said, "it's an easy mistake to make. I must say you are the absolute spitting image of my old friend." He turned to the seated woman who had been watching the whole thing through narrow, suspicious eyes. "Enjoy the remainder of the game Madam, I have the feeling your luck may be about to change." With that he turned on his heel and walked away, leaving Twister looking considerably more disheveled and still clutching his arm.

"What did you just do?" Adam asked Grimble as he reached them.

"I thought that golden boy over there was too good to be true," Grimble replied with a grim smile. "He was pulling out just the right card at just the right time far too often. I had been keeping a really close eye on his hands as he played. Years of playing against this lanky trickster...," he nodded at Lucid, "... made me pretty good at that."

Lucid just tutted noncommittally, but with a half-smile that made Adam think he was more flattered than insulted by the comment.

"After a while, I realised that he wasn't being naturally lucky or particularly skilful, but he did seem to be in the habit of flexing his hand ever so slightly just before bringing out a winning card. I suspected he had some sort of gadget or device up his sleeve that was dropping the gambit card right into his palm just when he needed it. When I grabbed his arm just now, I could clearly feel some sort of mechanism under his sleeve."

He gave a cheerfully unpleasant smile. "Unfortunately, I must have squeezed his arm a bit too hard just now and think that I must have broken his device. Shame... I expect it was really expensive." His grin broadened, and he turned his attention back to the table where the game had re-commenced.

Twister wasn't looking anywhere near as confident and relaxed as he had been just a few minutes before. While Grimble had been explaining himself to his companions it looked like Twister had tried to end the game, claiming the onset of an extremely sudden and unexpected bout of sickness. But his opponent wasn't having any of it, nor were the crowd, who could sense that something was going on and were now gathered even more densely around the table, keen to see how things were going to play out.

With extremely bad grace Twister re-took his seat at the table, but instead of his previous relaxed slouch he was hunched forward over the table, staring intently at each card as it was played. It very quickly became clear that the tide of 'luck' had turned, with the next few hands all going to the tall woman, the pile of treasures slowly shifting from its spot in front of Twister to a new, and growing heap of winnings by her. Every few hands Twister would manage a win, but his confidence had completely gone, plus he seemed to be suffering some discomfort with his right arm, and within a surprisingly short time he was down to his last few trinkets.

It took just one final hand for the woman to claim the last few treasures on the table, for once playing the Gambit card herself, just as she had secured enough of a lead to guarantee the win.

With scarcely concealed disgust Twister pushed his chair back from the table and stalked off, still clutching his right arm. He gave one final, vitriolic glare over his shoulder, straight at Grimble, and then he vanished off into the crowds.

"I think we may need to watch our backs from now on," Lucid told Grimble, staring across at the spot where the Sornette Card Sharp had left the barge. "He might be a bit of a dandy on the surface, but your new friend is a dangerous character."

"Bah, let him try," Grimble replied, then nodded in the direction of the one remaining player sat at the table, "for the moment we have more pressing priorities."

Now that the spectacle of the game was over, the crowd was rapidly thinning, and after a couple of minutes there were only a few stragglers left, everyone else having wandered off to find a new source of entertainment.

"So, what do you want?" the woman asked, looking up from the table as the three of them approached her. "I know you did something to that card sharp... which I appreciate... I really do, but now I presume you want something from me in return."

Her words were friendly enough, but there was a resigned weariness in her voice that made Adam think she was unused to receiving help without there being some bigger price to pay. He thought back to Lucid's visit with Granny and her fondness of being owed favours, wondering how much went on below the surface of Reverie.

Adam nodded. "You're right," he said, "there is something, but it was something of mine that Twister had stolen. It wasn't his to use in the first place." He pointed at the pendant, nestled in the middle of a pile of shinier treasures.

"Is that it?" she asked, obviously surprised that he had picked what looked like the least valuable item on the table.

"It means a lot to me," Adam told her, as she picked up the pendant and dangled it by the chain between two of her long metal fingers, giving it a final quizzical look before handing it to him.

"Thank you," Adam said, wasting no time in refastening the pendant's chain around his neck, pretty sure he could feel a pulse of welcoming warmth against his chest as he did so. "Pleased to meet you, by the way, I'm Adam and these are my friends Lucid and Grimble."

Adam extended his hand politely as he finished his introductions. He tried not to wince involuntarily as the cold metal fingers of the woman's hand closed around his, but when she shook his hand it was far gentler than he had expected.

"Isabella Farthing," she replied, meeting his querying look with a steady gaze of her own. One of her eyes was a flat, rather murky hazel colour, but the other was a piercing green that shone in the light of the table lamps. Despite this, the hazel eye was the one that held the tiniest spark of warmth, while the other remained completely lifeless. Realising he was staring Adam looked away, embarrassed.

"I don't believe it," he heard Lucid mutter behind him. "Did you say your name was Farthing?"

"Yes, what of it," the woman replied curtly, releasing her grip on Adam's hand and absentmindedly straightening her cuff, pulling it down as far as possible over the exposed metal of her hand.

"You are the woman we are looking for," Lucid continued. "Isabella Farthing, sea captain, explorer, adventurer..."

"...and stark raving bonkers troublemaker, or so the rumours suggest" Grimble added with a growl.

Her lips curved into a twisted grin at this last comment. "Seems that my fame precedes me." Then her smile vanished as quickly as it had appeared and her eyes narrowed in suspicion. "So how do you know my name and why are you looking for me?"

"We need a ship... and a captain capable of sailing across the Dwam," Lucid quickly explained, "and we were told that you were pretty much the only person skilled enough..."

"...or crazy enough," Grimble added, which only seemed to amuse the woman more.

She gave a short barking laugh. "I was only here in the first place because my ship needed repair, and now..." she looked across at the treasures that were still heaped on the table, "...now I have all the threads I need to get my girl back in full working order."

"So, are you and your ship available to hire?" Lucid asked, trying his hardest to make the question sound casual, and managing to fail completely.

Isabella sighed. "I would normally, by which I mean absolutely always, say most definitely not... but I'm pretty sure that it's only because of your interference that I didn't lose the last of my belongings."

She walked back across to the table and pulled a small bag from her coat pocket, stopping only to sweep the pile of treasures and trinkets into it, whistling to herself cheerfully as she did.

"I have enough of these sparkly little trinkets, knick-knacks, and what-nots to pay for all of my repairs and more... so I will make you a deal." She turned back to face them, slinging her new bag of treasures over one shoulder. "You tell me why you want to cross the Dwam, the real reason mind, not some made up excuse, then I will... consider hiring you my ship, my knowledge, and my time.

Grimble shot Adam a warning glance, but something about this strange woman rang true with him. She had already returned his pendant without a fuss, and despite her rather brusque nature, he had an overwhelming feeling that behind the cynical exterior was someone he could trust. A feeling which he hoped he wasn't about to regret.

"We need to go to the place where the Nightmares come from," Adam began, waiting to hear a snort of derision or some other outcry of disbelief. Instead of this Isabella was looking at him with interest glimmering in her good eye.

"Why would you want to go there? It is a terrible place... or so they say," Isabella asked, her gaze flitting between Adam and his two companions. Lucid was watching the conversation rather nervously, whereas Grimble's face was stony and expressionless, a far cry from the flamboyant character he had been playing only a few minutes before.

"I think that my mum is there," Adam said, trying to keep his voice neutral. "I have been looking for her for a long time, and I was told that is where I need to look... if I ever want to find her."

"Well, you're brave, I will give you that," Isabella said, steepling her fingers and then stretching them out in front of her, her brass fingers interlocking with the dark skin of her other hand. "And foolhardy," she continued, "both of which are character traits I see all too rarely. Besides which I quite fancy doing something interesting before I die, and the voyage you are suggesting will make sure I get to do just that."

"Do you mean that this will give you something interesting to do, or that this journey will mean certain death," Grimble muttered, only half to himself, but Isabella didn't respond.

"I will meet you across at the eastern dock first light tomorrow," she told them, "and by the way, my friends call me Bella"

"So, we're all good friends now, are we?" Grimble asked.

"No," Bella replied, "but after you pay me I am sure we will get on just fine. I will see you all again in the morning... and don't be late."

With that parting shot she left Adam and his friends, strolling away in her slightly uneven rolling gait.

"It's been an odd sort of day," Adam managed, not really having the right words to explain how he felt. He had gone from the depths of despair, convinced he has lost his pendant and his last link to his mother, to his current elation, having found a possible way to cross the Dwam.

"Happy as I am that things have worked out so well, and that we now have a plan for tomorrow, tonight we really need to find somewhere to stay," Lucid said, bringing the conversation back to a more normal topic. "It's a long time till dawn and I don't fancy sleeping in the open, or back on the Dreamskipper if I can help it. If we have a long and uncomfortable journey ahead of us, then a final night in a decent bed doesn't seem too much to ask."

However, finding a decent bed turned out to be more of a challenge than they first hoped. The Grand Assembly had attracted visitors from all over Reverie, and every one of the floating inns within the temporary gathering seemed to be full. These ranged from what looked like reasonably professional establishments to much more makeshift affairs, obviously lashed together at short notice by barge owners who had seen the opportunity to make some quick money.

They were beginning to lose hope that they would find anywhere to stay, about to give it up as a lost cause and return to the Dreamskipper, when they were disturbed by a surprised, but very cheerful shout of welcome.

"Lucid! Lucid what are you doing here?"

There, stood slightly in the shadows, was a figure that Adam recognised, and which was immediately familiar to Lucid.

"Tremello!" Lucid shouted back in delight, raising his hand in greeting to the tall, slender, silhouetted figure now approaching them with outstretched arms.

After a brief, affectionate hug, which unusually even Grimble didn't try to avoid, Tremello took a step back and gave the group a calculating look, her hands resting on slim hips.

"So, what's going on this time then?" she asked them, her eyebrow arched so high that it nearly vanished under the brim of her cheerily decorated bowler hat. "Whenever I see you there is something going on... is the world about to end again?"

Although her tone remained playful Adam could see that there was a hint of genuine concern behind the smile, and for a moment he was consumed by guilty memories. He could almost feel the heat of the flames and hear the crackle of burning barges sounding again in his ears, as he and his friends had fled from Isenbard's attack. Back then, before he had realised what he was capable of, Tremello and her fellow Sornette had helped Adam and his companions escape from a terrible ambush, and the Sornette had paid a heavy price as a result.

Although the majority of the barges had eventually been saved, Adam still wondered if he could have saved them all, if only he had managed to master his Daydreaming abilities earlier. When his attention returned to the present, Lucid was part way through explaining their current adventures to Tremello.

"So, you came here to find a sea-captain?" Tremello asked.

"Exactly," Lucid nodded, "and by very great fortune, or some intervention by the Dreamer himself, we managed to find one... perhaps the only one who can make the journey we need to undertake."

"Which is?"

Lucid shuffled his feet uncomfortably on the spot for a moment. Adam could tell he was desperate to share the full story with Tremello, but at the same time it was clear that Lucid also hadn't managed to fully leave behind the guilt of the last time he had spent time with his people. If anything, he felt the weight of responsibility for what had happened to them even more acutely than Adam.

"I probably shouldn't say any more," he told her, with his eyes slightly downcast. "It could be dangerous... I mean dangerous for you... to know too much about what we are planning."

"I'll leave that decision up to you," Tremello said brightly, although Adam could sense the hurt behind her cheerful smile. "But whatever your plans, I presume you are not heading out tonight?"

Lucid nodded. "That's true. We leave in the morning, but for the moment we were looking for somewhere to stay."

"Which hasn't been going very well, to be honest," Adam admitted.

Tremello's smile broadened. "Then you must stay with us, several of our barges have moored up amongst the Grand Assembly, this year we have quite a sizable delegation. The Maman is here too, she has a number of important trading arrangements that she is looking to finalise." She stopped for a moment, then added, with a knowing wink in Lucid's direction, "for some reason she seems to think that trade with Moonshine is likely to be a particularly promising new area to explore."

Although Lucid blushed slightly he didn't say anything, and despite his obvious fondness towards Tremello, Adam got the sneaking feeling that he was not completely happy with the invitation to join her and the rest of his clan for the night.

Still, he didn't turn the offer down, and after a few more minutes of small talk, Lucid, Adam and Grimble were following Tremello from barge to barge.

As they moved across the gathering Adam realised that there was an underlying pattern to the way the barges were laid out. He started to notice little details, like the fact that the colourful canopies and flags on the barges had dominant colours and patterns which seemed to be specific to different clans.

Tremello paused as she crossed a final makeshift bridge onto the deck of one of the bigger barges with a series of large, tent-like structures erected across it, swathes of dark blue material dotted with golden moons and stars splashed across the majority.

"I think we can find enough room to squeeze you in here," Tremello told them, pointing to the nearest of the tents. "Perhaps I'll see you later?" she added, although this final comment was clearly aimed at Lucid.

"Yes... most probably," Lucid gave her a brief smile before lifting the flap of the tent and ducking through the entrance. Inside the tent was more spacious than it had looked from the outside, with a row of comfortable looking beds along one side, and a small table and a set of chairs providing an informal eating area on the other. Grimble wasted no time in picking out a bunk and settling himself down, presumably with no intention of moving for the rest of the night. His intentions became even more clear when, within a few minutes, the tent began to reverberate with determined snoring.

Adam found another bunk and tried to get off to sleep himself, knowing he should take the chance to get back to the 'real' world and, amongst other things, start revising for his maths test.

Unfortunately, every time he was about to drift off to sleep a particularly violent snore from Grimble would jerk him rudely awake again. Eventually, giving the whole thing up as a bad job, Adam wearily got back out of his bed, deciding to have a wander out on the deck and see if some fresh air would help.

He wasn't completely surprised to see that he wasn't the only one out on deck. In the times he had spent with them, Adam had found the Sornette to be a pretty nocturnal bunch, often dancing, playing music and telling tales into the early hours of the morning.

There was no music or dancing tonight on the barge, but there were several tall figures silhouetted against the glow coming from a large, copper fire pit stood in the centre of the deck. Adam walked across, attracted by the warmth of flames, and was pleased to see one of the closest figures was Tremello. She was sat near to the fire, chin resting on her hands and eyes staring into the flames, so she didn't spot Adam until he'd nearly reached her.

"Hello Adam," she said, patting the cushion next to her, "have a seat."

"Hi Tremello, I thought you would be talking with Lucid to be honest. I didn't see him in the tent, so I presumed…"

"Hah," she gave a slightly bitter laugh. "Your friend is infuriating. He's probably off moping somewhere rather than talking with me like he promised."

"Moping?" Adam replied in surprise, he couldn't imagine Lucid, with his ever-ready smile, doing anything like that, but Tremello seemed pretty serious.

He took a seat next to her, letting the waves of warm air from the glowing coals of the fire pit wash over him.

"So, what's the matter?" Adam asked.

"I keep telling him that he is welcome here, but he is so stubborn," Tremello said, half to herself.

"He always seems so happy to see you, and I know he was excited about coming to the Grand Assembly." Adam said, "I don't understand why he would be avoiding you now?"

"Look," Tremello said, turning away from the fire and facing Adam directly. "I don't know if I should really tell you all of this, but… you and Lucid seem like you're close and perhaps… perhaps you can talk some sense into him."

"Um..." Adam settled for a non-committal grunt, torn between loyalty to his friend and having to admit he was intrigued to find out what Tremello was talking about.

Taking this as agreement Tremello settled back in her chair.

"To understand why Lucid finds it hard to see me... to see us all, you need to understand about his past. We grew up together, raised on the same barge and for those first years of his life he didn't know anything else. Then the call came for one of us to join the Five. As you no doubt know, the Five normally has representation from each of the races of Reverie."

Adam nodded, he remembered the portraits in the Mansion and the painting with Lucid's predecessor, a narrow faced Sornette named Spindle, who had fallen while fighting a previous Horror.

"After Spindle was lost, we were asked to send a replacement to the city, to take his place. Lucid's head was always full of stories of adventure and so, unsurprisingly he jumped at the chance. Quite a few of the younger Sornette wanted to take the opportunity, me included. We saw it as a way to see the world, to have adventures, rather than just telling stories about them around the fire."

Tremello picked up a mug from the small table between the seats and took a quick sip.

"Do you want one?" she asked, offering Adam a mug of his own.

He nodded gratefully. The mug was steaming gently, and although the taste was initially a little bitter, Adam soon got used to the flavour and found it pleasantly warming. Settling back into his own chair he listened as Tremello continued her tale.

"We should have prepared him better, he was keen and very, very bright, but he had never been away from the Sornette and Reverie has its... challenges." Tremello was staring into the fire and Adam got the impression that she was wandering through the back-streets of her memories, hardly aware that he was even there.

"He ran into trouble, more than he was able to talk his way out of. He should have come back to us, we could have helped him if he asked... but he didn't."

47

Images of Granny's cruel smile swam back to the front of Adam's mind, mixed in with memories of the simmering anger he had seen in Lucid after their meeting.

"Rather than come back or admitting he was out of his depth, he got in with some very bad people. I still don't know exactly what happened after that, he has never told me... as far as I know he has never told anyone." She pulled her attention back from whatever time or place it had been inhabiting and looked across at Adam with the unspoken question hanging heavily between them.

"I don't know either," Adam admitted. "He hasn't told me, and if he ever told Grimble then he hasn't shared it either."

Sighing to herself, not seeming particularly surprised that Adam couldn't shed any extra light on Lucid's time in Reverie, Tremello resumed her story.

"Whatever it was, it came between us. I don't know if he was ashamed of the trouble that he had gotten into, of the company he ended up having to keep, or whether it was something else, something more, but he has been distant ever since. On occasion he would still visit, join us from time to time at some gathering or another, but behind his smile there was always a barrier up somewhere within him. We miss him... I miss him."

"I think he misses you too," Adam told her, noticing the tiny spark of hope in her eyes as he spoke. "On our journey to visit you the first time, life on the barges was all he talked about... and I have honestly never seen him happier than when he saw you up on the deck. Even this time, although I could tell something wasn't quite right with him, he was so excited about the Grand Assembly that he could hardly stand still."

"I know you have to leave early tomorrow," Tremello said, plucking one of the small dried flowers from the cluster tied around her bowler hat. "I might not see him again before he goes... so could you give him this from me... for luck."

Hardly feeling he could refuse, and hoping that he could find a way to make the small token seem as important to Lucid tomorrow as it felt to him now, Adam took the flower and tucked it safely inside his pocket. "Of course," he replied. "I'll make sure he gets it."

With all the important things that needed to be said now spoken, they sat together for a few minutes longer in companionable silence, finishing their drinks, and then Tremello stood and waggled her fingers in a friendly goodbye. "Safe travels Daydreamer. May the Weave always carry you home."

Lucid's bed was still empty when Adam returned to the tent, presumably still off wandering the decks of the Grand Assembly. Although he wanted to stay awake until Lucid came back, determined to pass across Tremello's message, eventually tiredness caught up with him and Adam left the Dream World behind once again.

CHAPTER 5

Back in the Waking World, far from the Grand Assembly, the Sornette, and any kind of adventure but infinitely closer to other dangers, particularly the looming menace of maths exams, Nora was feeling extremely frustrated, as she had pretty much every day since she had returned from Reverie. Her means of entering the Dream World had disappeared without warning when the friendly Nightmare, (as far as it was possible for a Nightmare to be described as friendly), who had stayed with her ever since her first visit, had suddenly decided to leave.

Nora had hoped, she now realised rather optimistically, that she would still somehow be able to travel to and from the Dream World when she slept, even without Mittens' help, (Mittens being the entirely inappropriate name that she had decided to give to the Nightmare. A name which had, against all the odds, stuck).

Unfortunately, this hadn't turned out to be the case and, instead of helping as she wanted to, she had found herself limited to hearing about the events taking place in Reverie second-hand whenever she got the chance to chat privately with Adam.

Having been instrumental in saving Adam, and most probably all of the Dream World the last time she had been there, returning to her normal day to day routine was proving to be almost unbearable. The resulting frustration had started spilling out in angry outbursts or sudden fits of tears that were completely out of character.

Adam had once again managed to get on the wrong side of Miss. Grudge during the morning lessons. He was obviously tired, with heavy bags under his eyes and had paid little attention to anything Miss. Grudge had been trying to teach. Unsurprisingly he was now stuck in yet another lunchtime detention session, although Nora did have the sneaking thought that he probably had deserved it this time, which had left Nora and Charlie to spend their lunch break without him.

However this time, rather than choosing to sit with Nora as he often did when Adam wasn't around, Charlie, possibly still stung by the way she had ignored him and Adam the day before, had chosen to sit on his own. She could see he was trying desperately not to make any sort of eye contact with her, although still looking up several times a minute to make sure she could see that he was ignoring her.

Refusing stubbornly to give him the satisfaction of acknowledging this, Nora chose to eat her lunch on her own rather than approach him. Munching through her sandwiches particularly aggressively didn't make her feel any better, her mood only worsening when she squeezed her bag of crisps too hard, popping the bag and exploding shards of crisp across the table.

Tying to ignore the laughs from the nearest tables, a blush running up her neck and across her cheeks, Nora walked from the dinner hall. Her fists were clenched, fingernails pressed into the palms of her hands, but she managed to resist the almost overwhelming desire to run or look across to see if Charlie was watching.

Sat in her room later that evening Nora kept replaying the scene in the dining hall over and over in her head, fresh feelings of embarrassment bubbling to the surface every time she thought of it. She knew it was ridiculous, she had faced down monsters and nightmare creatures, and was pretty sure she had saved a world, or at least a city, so the laughter of a few school kids shouldn't bother her at all. But somehow it was harder, not easier, to cope with.

She looked down at her wrist, at the spot where Mittens had wrapped herself, (when she wasn't causing trouble), their last conversation worming its way back into the forefront of her mind. "You said that I would be okay, you said that some doors, once opened were hard to close again." She sighed, rubbing her wrist, "but I can't open the door back to Reverie, no matter how hard I try."

That night, the same as every night for the last few weeks, she closed her eyes with images of Reverie locked firmly in mind, desperate to find her way back, but all that she found was empty, dreamless sleep.

That night when Adam dropped into his bed in the Henson's spare room, exhausted by the constant cycle of days and nights spent alternately in the Waking World and the Dream World, it was extremely tempting to just let blissful, adventure-free sleep fill his night for once. He had been so tired that he'd felt like he was walking through a thick fog most of the day, separating him and his sleepy brain from the rest of the world. Every conversation felt like it was through a wall of cotton wool, muffled and unclear, every action like he was weighed down, walking through the world in an old-fashioned diver's suit. Still, there was no way he could stop at the moment. He was well on his way to finding his mum and until that happened, he wouldn't allow himself the luxury of a genuine night of rest.

When he woke in Reverie again, he found himself back on the deck of the Dreamskipper. It looked like his companions had made an early start and that they were already well on their way back to Nocturne. Stood at the far end of the barge, looking off into the distance was the tall, dark figure of Isabella. If the sight of a boy suddenly materialising on the deck surprised her, she didn't let it show, just greeting Adam with a languid wave of her brass fingers as if it was the kind of thing that happened to her all the time.

Lucid wasted no time bringing Adam up to date. "Apparently Bella has sent a message ahead of us, to the yardman repairing her ship. Hopefully, by the time we get back to Nocturne, most of the repairs will be complete and we can make preparations for our departure."

Despite his apparent enthusiasm Lucid looked and sounded nearly as tired as Adam, dark circles under his eyes and his voice deeper and hoarser than normal. Adam wondered if he had even made it back to his bed the previous night. Remembering his promise to Tremello, he rooted around in his pockets, pulling out the dried flower. Bella was still stood at the opposite end of the barge and Grimble was currently out of sight, most likely hiding himself away in the small cabin, so it seemed like a good time to pass across Tremello's message without embarrassing Lucid any more than necessary.

"Before I forget, this is for you," Adam said, handing the small flower across. It had held its shape remarkably well, considering how long it had spent nestled away in his pocket, and Adam could tell that Lucid recognised it immediately.

"Tremello said to give you this... for luck," Adam told his friend, who had taken the flower gently between slender fingers and was looking down at it with an expression that Adam found hard to interpret. He looked happy, but there was still an underlying sense of sadness that poked through, like the finest of cracks in a porcelain vase, almost invisible but with the potential to one day break the whole thing if left unrepaired.

Not really knowing what to say, Adam used the same approach he applied to most things, he dived straight in and hoped for the best. "Tremello says that she misses you."

Lucid flinched slightly at the words, as if Adam had said something hurtful, then his expression softened again and his shoulders slumped. "I miss her too... I miss all of them, but sometimes you have to make hard choices... and pay the price for those choices."

"I don't think she cares about whatever it was that happened before... I don't think she even knows... she just wanted to let you know that she misses you and wants the best for you. I think the flower was to remind you of that."

Lucid didn't say anything in response, but Adam saw him tuck the flower into the band of his top hat, snuggled in amongst the other oddities he kept there, then he turned and walked back across the deck to join Bella.

She was standing with her hands gripping the rail at the front of the barge, her face and upper body leaning forward over the rail, as if she was so keen to reach their destination that even a few centimetres mattered.

She didn't say anything as Lucid and Adam joined her, just nodded companionably, then returned her gaze to the horizon. Adam could see the brass fingers of her right arm tapping out a gentle, but insistent and impatient tempo.

This impatience to reach their destination became increasingly pronounced when they finally reached the bustling dockyards of Nocturne. Even Lucid, with his naturally lanky frame and long legs, struggled to keep up with her uneven stride once she was off the Dreamskipper and walking across the docks. The crowds that Adam generally had to thread his way through appeared to part in front of her as she cut a direct line from one end of the docks to the other. It seemed that Bella had earned a reasonable amount of either respect or fear from the day to day inhabitants of the docks, while in turn treating the crowds around her with complete indifference.

The only individual who did briefly get in her way was a solitary dreamer, a businessman being chased through the docks by a flock of umbrellas, flapping open and closed like giant, water-resistant bats. Just as Bella reached him a couple of the umbrellas caught up with the unfortunate fellow and hooking their handles under his belt slowly lifted him into the air, although his legs continued to pedal uselessly as he was carried away.

Grimble and Adam were pretty much running by the time they reached their destination, not helped by the fact that the crowds that had parted for Bella and Lucid seemed to reform again just behind them, leaving Adam and Grimble to jostle their way through. On several occasions, it was only the sight of Lucid's top hat bobbing away in the distance that meant they didn't lose them completely.

The area of the docks they found themselves in was one of the less salubrious districts, not exactly disreputable, but also not one which you would brag about. Most of the buildings looked as if they only remained standing out of stubbornness, hanging on to honour the memory of previous and more successful times; when the trades and craftsman that had filled them had been the pinnacle of what Nocturne had to offer.

It was at one of these buildings, a slightly ramshackle shed with a sign hanging off a cast-iron bracket proudly declaring the place to be 'Jim's Excellent Boat and Ship Repairs' that Bella had stopped. Running along the left-hand-side of the building there was a long, wooden walkway leading out into the shallow mists of the Weave, which swirled gently around the sturdy supporting posts driven at forty-five-degree angles into the muddy banks that lined it.

It was down this that Bella now walked, her impatient stride slowing now she had reached her destination.

"Jim!" she shouted, "where are you and how is my girl?"

Without waiting for a reply, she carried on down the walkway and turned around the far corner of the building. As Adam followed her, he was greeted by a fascinating sight. There, moored in a shallow dock directly behind the building was one of the oddest vessels that he had ever seen.

Up until now, the only boats he had seen in Reverie had been the shallow barges of the Sornette or the rather more mechanical but similarly shaped vessels that Chimera had operated. The ship that Adam was looking at now was nothing like any of those. The hull was gently curved, almost oval in shape, formed of a dark wood banded with metal strips and lifting gently out of the Weave at both the bow and the stern. The ship's name, 'the Mayfly' was painted on the side in bold white letters, while on the deck there was a central mast with a complicated looking set of ropes and pulleys splaying out on all sides. To Adam, the whole thing looked rather like an over-turned woodlouse.

Hanging off one side of the boat, in a makeshift harness dangling from the mast, welding a metal panel into place was a small figure wearing thick overalls and dark goggles that obscured most of his face. Every now and then he would pause his welding to frantically pat down his clothing where a stray spark had caught fire.

After a few minutes, during which Bella had paced up and down the wooden walkway with increasingly obvious impatience, the figure finished his work, painstakingly winched his way down from the side of the vessel and then unclipped himself from the harness.

55

After removing the heavy gauntlets he wiped his hands absentmindedly on the stained front of the overalls and then lifted the goggles from his eyes, pushing them high onto his forehead.

"All done," he said to Bella, not paying Adam or his friends any attention. "I got the message late in the evening and have been working all night... not that I owe you any f...fa...favours after the last time we spoke, but at least you'll leave me in peace now." He paused and tugged nervously at his beard. "You w...wi...will leave me alone now won't you?"

"I think that we're all square now Jim," Bella said, handing him across a bag that jangled heavily with the majority of the treasures she had won. Adam's concern that such a random mixture of items would be considered suitable as payment was short-lived, as Jim rummaged busily through the bag, giving the occasional exclamation of interest as one item or another caught his attention.

"Yes, this will do... this will do very nicely." Jim closed the bag, tying the top tightly closed, then his expression turned stony. "And now I would thank you to get on your b...bo...boat, sail away and never, ever bother me again..."

CHAPTER 6

The journey from the docks of Nocturne to the closest shores of the Dwam was expected to take much longer than a full day's travel, and Adam agreed with Lucid and the others that he would join them once they were ready to start their journey across the great sea. Fortunately, the next day back at home was Saturday, which meant that he could sleep late in the morning.

Adam took full advantage of the chance to rest for once, not emerging from the Henson's spare room until mid-morning. It also meant that he was at no risk of getting himself in trouble at school, and as Charlie's mum and dad were out, he would have some time to properly catch up with Charlie on everything that had been happening.

"Bit late for breakfast mate," Charlie said, briefly pausing his determined munching of his eighth (or possibly even ninth) slice of post-breakfast toast, when Adam finally made it into the kitchen. "To be honest you're nearly too late for dinner as well. Mum was starting to worry that you were ill, but I set her straight and said you were fine... just really lazy."

"Thanks," Adam grunted, letting his head slump down onto the breakfast table. "Still... so... tired... this is ridiculous."

"Literally zero sympathy. If you will spend all the time when you should be sleeping whooshing around a dream world and fighting evil or whatever it is you keep doing, then you only have yourself to blame." Charlie walked across to the radio and clicked it on, filling the room with a particularly loud and catchy pop song that grated on Adam's exhausted brain like a cat scratching a blackboard.

"I hate you," Adam managed, wiggling his fingers in the direction of the radio and wishing that he could use his Daydreaming in the

Waking World. He wasn't sure if it was considered an acceptable use of his powers to destroy radios, but at the moment he didn't care. It didn't make any difference anyway, with the tiny speaker continuing to pump out its agonizingly chirpy tune.

Taking pity on his friend, Charlie turned the radio back off. "Fine, I'll be nice this time. You do look pretty rough, perhaps you need a day... or night off. You won't be any good to anyone if your brain implodes from lack of sleep."

"Can that happen?" Adam asked. "At the moment I kind of hope it could, at least it would get rid of my headache." He grimaced and smacked his lips a couple of times, "plus my mouth tastes like I've tried to chew a camel to death... a really, really ill camel."

By the middle of the afternoon, Adam had managed to shake off the worst of his headache and decided to try and make use of his free time by going to see Nora. Despite his previous failures he hadn't given up on trying to rebuild some of their recently burnt bridges. The walk to her house was spent updating Charlie on the latest from Reverie, with Charlie having decided that he would accompany Adam on his visit to provide some much-needed moral support.

By the time they reached Nora's front door, Adam had got as far as explaining about Bella and the Mayfly.

"Sounds like you're mixed up with even odder characters than normal... which is saying something," Charlie said, as Adam rang the doorbell.

"Bella's a bit unusual, but it seems like she's my best chance of crossing the sea and finding my mum."

Adam rang the bell again and then peered up at the front window to Nora's room. The curtains were firmly closed, although he could have sworn that he'd seen the corner of one twitch slightly just as he had looked up.

"Come on Nora... I know you're in." But despite his insistent ringing, the front door remained firmly closed and the curtain didn't move again.

"Never mind mate, maybe we can wait around a bit and see if she comes back later?" Charlie said, with a reassuring smile.

Adam looked sadly up at Nora's window one last time. "I don't think that she is coming back any time soon. We might as well go back home."

That night it took longer than normal for Adam to get to sleep. Normally, despite whatever excitement he might be feeling about re-entering the Dream World, he didn't find it hard to drop off in the comfort of his bed and find his way back into Reverie, but he was finding it hard to settle his mind. Every time he was close to drifting away, he would think back to Nora's closed curtains, certain that she had been sat there alone in her room, refusing to answer the door.

That thought was still spinning unwanted within his brain when he finally managed to sleep.

CHAPTER 7

The deck was hard and uncomfortable under his back when Adam woke back in Reverie, which didn't do much to help his mood.

A friendly slap on the back from Grimble as he clambered rather wearily to his feet was similarly unhelpful, nearly knocking him back over.

"You made it then," Grimble said. "I wasn't sure if you would find it as easy to reach us, out in the middle of the sea... but it doesn't seem to have caused you any problems."

In all honesty, Adam's brain had been so full of worries about his rapidly deteriorating relationships back in the Waking World, that he hadn't really thought too deeply about finding his way back to his friends in Reverie. The fact that they were now sat somewhere on the great sea of dreams, the Dwam, didn't seem to have made any difference, and he had found his way to them almost without thinking.

The Mayfly seemed bigger than he remembered it looking in the small dock in Nocturne and he spent a few minutes finding his way around. The central mast still looked every bit as complex when viewed up close, with all manner of winches, pulleys and unexplained additions hanging off it, so he was especially careful not to touch it.

At the back was a reasonably sized cabin, with two sets of bunks, one against each side. In the centre of the room, halfway between the bunks, there was a table, just large enough to seat four. Finally, against the back wall, there was a small but well-organised workbench, with a selection of cogs, bolts, springs and neatly labelled oil-cans in the racks just underneath.

Back out on the deck, Bella showed him the hatch that led into the ship's hold. The majority was currently empty, although to one side there were several crates of supplies which Bella had stocked specifically for the voyage. Adam could see food, bottled water and a few items of specialised looking equipment that he didn't recognise.

His quick tour complete, Adam joined the others where they had gathered around the small table back in the cabin.

"So how long will it take to reach the land of Nightmares?" he asked Bella.

"Honestly, I don't know," she replied. "I have been close, but never quite reached those far shores in my previous travels."

"What in the great dream even made you travel so far... to risk going so close to the Nightmares?" snorted Grimble.

"I have travelled these oceans for most of my adult life," Bella told them, with an underlying lilt to her voice that made Adam realise, without doubt, that she hadn't regretted a single minute of that time. "But despite that, despite all the knowledge that I have gained, beyond that of pretty much anyone else in the whole of Reverie, there are still some mysteries that the Dwam holds... and the Deep Sleeper is one of those. My search for her has taken me all over this ocean, including the seas closest to the land of the Nightmares."

"I thought that the Deep Sleeper was a myth," Lucid said, eyebrows raised about as far as they could go on his high forehead.

"She is," replied Bella, not in the least perturbed. "She is a myth... a legend... a monster to scare children, telling them tales of the big bad creature that swims deep in the Dwam." She leant forward, resting her elbows on the table. "And she is also the single most real thing in the whole of Reverie. The greatest adventure of my life has been searching for her. I have caught up with her twice in all those years." She paused, flexing the brass fingers of her right hand. "One of those times cost me my arm, the other my leg."

"And also your eye I suppose?" Grimble cut in tersely.

"No," Bella smiled back at him, apparently quite used to her comments being met with disbelief. "That was the result of an unfortunate misunderstanding with a bar full of rather rowdy Sornette traders, who seemed to think I owed them money... which I did as it happens. Their mistake was thinking that I was going to pay them back."

"Why do you keep looking?" Adam asked her. "Sooner or later you're going to run out of bits you can spare."

"Sadly, I can't really help myself." Bella turned her attention back to Adam as she spoke. "I have always looked for adventure, generally on my own. No offence to you and your friends but most of the time I can't really be doing with other people. They are always so... disappointing."

She lifted her hands from the table and spread her arms wide as if embracing the whole of the Dwam. "And where better to adventure on your own than the Dwam, where no one in their right mind would ever venture." She sighed, not unhappily, but with the wistfulness of unfulfilled dreams. "And what better adventure can there be than to find the beast that rules the Dwam... the Deep Sleeper."

"And then what... do you mean to hunt it?" asked Lucid, obviously fascinated despite himself.

"No, absolutely not," Bella sounded horrified at the suggestion, "but they say that the skin of the Deep Sleeper is encrusted with thousands of crystals that have formed over the ages, tiny solidified pieces of the Dwam. I want one... just one of those for myself. Proof that there is something greater than all of us, older than all of us, out there."

Her previously melancholy tone returned to a more familiar light-heartedness as she concluded. "Besides I thought that one of those crystals would make an excellent replacement for this…" She leant her head back rummaging around with her good hand for a moment before flicking her glass eye up into the air and then catching it again nonchalantly. "Imagine having a piece of the Dwam for an eye, a millennia of crystalised dreams… imagine what you would see."

For a moment she stared at the glass orb held so casually in front of her, and then with her reminiscing over, Bella returned to the matter of their current voyage with a slightly embarrassed cough. "Anyway… enough of such talk. I would estimate, if fate is kind to us, we will reach the continent of the Nightmares within a week. The journey isn't particularly far, but it is treacherous, and across a stretch of the Dwam that almost no one has ever tried to cross."

A swirl of mist washed in through the cabin window and snaked its way across the room, circling the lantern hanging over the table before slowly dissipating.

"Speaking of fate being kind to us, it looks like a storm could be gathering," Grimble muttered, gripping the table edge. While he was putting a brave face on things, Adam knew that floating around in the middle of the Dwam was pretty much the last thing that Grimble would ever choose to do, and he felt a rush of gratitude that his friends were willing to risk so much just to help him.

"No problem," said Adam, "I can take a look," wanting to show his appreciation by helping out where he could. He stepped back out onto the deck and after briefly concentrating, summoned memories of dreams where he had been able to fly. Crouching down slightly, which was completely unnecessary but something that he had decided looked very cool, he launched himself into the air, planning to fly up above the boat to get a good look around. However, rather than the gentle climb he had planned, he shot into the air so fast that the rush of air passing his face stung his skin and made his eyes water.

Completely caught out by his uncontrolled rate of ascent he lost control of his direction, spiralling through the air like a gangly, panicking firework. By the time he managed to stop himself, arms outstretched unsteadily to either side, he was well above the clouds.

Trying to calm down and settle his breathing, he remembered when he had first tried his Daydreaming and had a similarly bad experience trying to fly back in the gardens of the Mansion. Still, a lot of time had passed since then and he was far more confident in his admittedly unusual abilities, so he couldn't understand why he had suddenly spun so far out of control.

Completely dropping any thoughts of having a look around, Adam instead peered down through the cloud trying to spot the Mayfly somewhere far below. Although it was now pin-prick tiny he was fairly sure he could see something amongst the misty waves of the Dwam. Taking a deep breath and aiming himself towards what he hoped was the ship he started to descend.

A couple of terrifying seconds of high-speed plummeting later and Adam managed to steady himself once again, now just a couple of hundred metres above the Mayfly and his crewmates, all of whom were staring up at him. He presumed he had made quite an unusual sight, bobbing around like a kite caught in strong winds. "What on earth is going on?" Adam muttered. It seemed almost impossible to control his movements. Every time he tried, it was like he was slamming his foot down on an internal accelerator or brake, going from zero to one-hundred miles an hour and back again with nothing in-between. Clenching his fists and concentrating as hard as he could, he picked a spot on the deck of the Mayfly that looked like it might provide a slightly softer landing spot than the rest, a pile of sacks gathered up close to the cabin.

"Right... slow, really, really slow," he muttered to himself. Unfortunately, the rest of the world didn't appear to be paying him any attention, and rather than the controlled descent he was desperately willing for himself, he dropped like a stone towards the deck. A couple of gut-wrenching seconds later and he crashed into the pile of sacks, landing much more heavily than he had planned and leaving him sure that he'd managed to break pretty much every part of his body.

Lying on his back and looking up through eyes misted over with the shock of his landing, a collection of concerned faces appeared over him.

"What in the Great Dream happened... are you all right?" Lucid asked.

Adam reached out and grasped his friend's hand, pleasantly surprised that his arm still seemed to be working.

"Ouch," he managed, adding another louder grunt of pain as Lucid pulled him onto his feet.

Now he was standing, Adam was able to check himself over more fully, and despite his first impressions, it seemed that nothing was broken, just very bruised.

"I don't know what happened," he said, wiggling his fingers and then cricking his neck, relieved that everything seemed to be working as it should. "It was like I couldn't control what I was doing, I'm just glad to be back down here in one piece."

"I think I might be able to explain," Grimble said, sitting down on one of the crates close to where Adam had landed. "I had my theories, and it looks like you have just proven them to be true. You remember how the Weave reacted to your powers before?"

Adam nodded, recalling the times when he had used his Daydreaming close to the Weave and the feeling of power he'd got from it, greatly increasing the strength of his dreams. Several times it had only been the Weave and the energy it had given him that had saved them all from disaster. Despite this, he also had to admit to himself that, on occasion, the resulting Daydreams had ended up

65

being both bigger and quite a bit more destructive than he had intended.

"Well, if the Weave intensifies the power of your dreams, to a point where I remember at least two buildings collapsing..." Grimble paused to shudder briefly, fingers running across the freshest of the scars that crisscrossed his face, "...just imagine what a whole ocean would do." He reached across and patted Adam on the arm. "I am afraid that it could be just too dangerous for you, and for the rest of us, if you use your powers anywhere on the Dwam. Even the smallest of your dreams could spiral totally out of control."

Walking across to the edge of the deck and looking over the side at the infinitely deep, swirling mists of the Dwam, Grimble grimaced. "And I don't fancy tempting fate any more than we need to, stuck in the middle of a massive sea of dreams with no land in sight." He snuck a sideways look at Bella. "Not to mention some giant sea monster paddling around somewhere. Actually, now I come to describe our situation, it sounds pretty bad even without out-of-control Daydreams being added to the mix."

Taking Grimble's advice to heart Adam spent the rest of the day sitting very quietly and calmly doing nothing, resisting the temptation to let his mind wander, just in case he managed to trigger a Daydream, even a tiny one, without meaning to.

The next few days passed in comparative calm, with Adam's time in the Waking World spent trying to cram in some revision for the upcoming and greatly dreaded maths exam. Charlie was working overtime on best friend duties, spending what seemed like an eternity going through possible maths questions with Adam, to the point where Adam felt like his head was going to explode and even Charlie's natural enthusiasm was flagging.

Every night when he fell asleep in the Henson's spare room he would wake on the deck of the Mayfly, spending most of his time in Reverie stood right at the front of the ship staring into the distance, desperate to see the first sight of land. It was increasingly hard to see far ahead, with the layer of mist hanging over the surface of the Dwam thickening the further they travelled. Adam could see now why they needed Bella so badly, the lack of visibility didn't seem to trouble her in the least. Every now and then she would look down at the small compass she kept in one of the pockets of her long trench-coat, make a small adjustment to their course, nod to herself and then settle back into her default position, leaning nonchalantly over the wheel of the Mayfly with a distant look in her good eye.

It was towards the end of their third full day of travel that Adam did spot something in the distance. "I can see something!" he shouted back to Bella, who shook her head in response.

"It shouldn't be land," she replied, "it's too soon."

Adam squinted into the mists, joined by Grimble and Lucid who had joined him at the front of the Mayfly for a better look. Rather than it being the first sight of land that Adam had been so hoping for, it was the prow of a huge and very decrepit ship that slowly emerged from the swirling haze. Adam had never seen anything quite like it.

Right at its front was a figurehead, which appeared to have been lashed to the prow with a variety of ropes, pulleys and randomly nailed planks. The figurehead itself looked like it was a brightly coloured animal of some kind with a golden coloured pole impaling it vertically, sticking out at least a couple of metres in either direction. It took a moment for Adam to realise what he was looking at. Then it struck him, it was a wooden horse which had been taken directly from a merry-go-round, explaining both the bright colours and the central pole. He was also pretty sure, despite all the connecting ropes and planks, that he could see the figurehead wobbling unsteadily as it approached them, looking like it could drop into the Dwam at any moment.

As the remainder of the ship emerged from the thick fog the oddness continued. The ship's sails, hanging rather limply from the huge central mast, were made of a variety of garishly coloured strips of material inexpertly stitched together. As with the figurehead Adam felt that the striped pattern of the sail was somehow familiar. He closed his eyes for a moment and his brain was almost immediately filled with images of clowns and greasepaint, acrobats and jugglers. More than anything else the sail reminded him of the brightly coloured stripes of a big top tent, although in this case there was a giant skull and crossbones daubed across it. "Pirates?" thought Adam to himself, still not entirely sure what he was looking at.

"I don't know whether I should feel scared or just confused," Lucid muttered as he stepped up alongside Adam, staring up at the strange vessel. "I didn't know that there was anyone else out here, let alone imagine running into something like that."

"Whatever this is, I doubt that it's a coincidence," said Grimble. "Out of all the great open space of the Dwam, where no one sane dares venture, that we should end up in this same, tiny section of the ocean..." he lowered his eyebrows in a suspicious scowl. "I think we should prepare ourselves for company."

Any further discussion was disturbed by a loud bang, matched with a bright glow directly above their heads. Adam's first reaction was to duck in panic, before realising that the glow had been caused by the sparkle of brightly coloured fireworks, sputtering and fizzing overhead and drenching them in tiny glimmering spots of gently burning dust. Before they had fully recovered from this strange assault, they were hailed from somewhere high on the larger vessel. "Stand by to be boarded!"

The speaker had a powerful and well-spoken voice. "Avast, landlubbers," they continued, "resist and we will have no choice but to... ahem... to slit your gizzards... Aarrr!" Although the voice remained strong, there was a very slight but unmistakable uncertainty weaved amongst their words, and Adam had the sneaking feeling that the speaker wasn't fully sure what they were saying.

There was swooshing sound and a figure dangling at the far end of a rope swung into view. From a distance Adam wondered what kind of creature it could be, silhouetted against the backdrop of the gaudy sail it seemed to have far too many arms and legs. Then as it drew closer Adam realised that it was, in fact, two figures, one hanging on to the others slim, outstretched arm. As the rope passed overhead both figures released their grip and plummeted down towards Adam and his companions, one of them performing an extravagant backflip in mid-air as they did so. Lucid dived with surprising grace out of the way, tucking his long limbs tightly into his body as he rolled, while Grimble simply stepped out of the way, tutting loudly to himself as one of the rapidly moving figures tumbled acrobatically past him.

Adam was left gawping open-mouthed, still trying to think what to do next, as the second of the figures placed a hand on his shoulder. He winced expecting the worst, instead of which the slim fingers merely gripped slightly more tightly for a moment as the shadowy silhouette flipped over his head, using his shoulder as a pivot.

There was a loud crash as a gangplank dropped down from the larger vessel onto the deck of the Mayfly, small splinters of wood scattering from the impact. Backlit against the luminous gloom of the sky, two large outlines made their way down the plank towards them. One incredibly tall and slim, the other wide and looming.

By this point, Lucid and Grimble had re-joined Adam in the centre of the deck and the three of them stood back-to-back watching the figures which now circled them. Bella was nowhere to be seen and Adam wondered where she had disappeared to at such a perilous moment.

The tallest of the approaching figures was dressed head to toe in a shiny, although slightly worn, black suit with a matching and extremely tall top hat, which made up at least a third of his total height. Pausing a few metres away he stood watching them with an imperious expression on his face, twiddling the end of a long and very well-oiled moustache.

To his immediate left was a huge rumbling mountain of a man, or at least Adam presumed he was a man unless a rhino had somehow managed to balance on its hind legs and dress itself in an extremely tight leotard. Out of consideration for their current activities, the leotard had a skull and crossbones spray-painted rather badly across the centre of its torso. Unfortunately, the leotard was so tight that every time the giant man moved or flexed a muscle it moved as well, the skull performing a number of gurning smiles and frowns.

To the other side were the two trapeze artists who had been the first to board the companion's ship, standing casually with slim limbs hanging loose and limber. The two women looked too similar for it to be a coincidence, the size, shape, and looks of one the exact mirror image of the other. "Twins," Adam muttered to himself. "Definitely twins... I bet they do all sorts of weird twin things like finishing each other sentences." In all honesty Adam didn't know any twins, but he had seen enough films to have developed a very firm set of opinions on the matter.

As the two groups stood watching each other, locked in the world's oddest Mexican standoff, there was a final loud bang from the larger vessel and a small shape span across between the ships, trailing smoke before landing with a crash almost directly between the two groups. "Ouch, ouch, ouch," the diminutive shape muttered, patting itself down as the last wisps of smoke died away.

Turning to face Adam the shape turned out to be a particularly small Drőmer, wearing a bright red crash helmet which appeared to be several sizes too large and a grubby white jumpsuit, emblazoned with a series of gold stars. Despite the helmet, he appeared slightly stunned by the recent landing and was swaying unsteadily.

After a few more seconds, which seemed to stretch on for much longer, during which a number of slightly embarrassed glances passed between the other odd intruders, the Drömer managed to clear his head slightly, dropped down to one knee and spread his arms wide with an exuberant "Ta-Dah!!"

"Right, now all the formalities are over, would you be so kind as to hand over your treasure and/or goods of value... um... me hearties," the top hat wearing man drawled. Adam was again unconvinced that the speaker was fully committed to what he was saying. If anything he sounded slightly... embarrassed by the whole thing.

"Nope, afraid that we can't help you," came a voice from just behind Adam. Bella was climbing out of the hold, fiddling with her mechanical arm as she did so. "Best I can do is offer you all a quick drink and wish you well on your journey."

The tall man frowned, then made an impatient gesture to the mountainous being next to him, who smacked one giant fist into an equally massive palm with an expectant grin before beginning to walk slowly towards Adam and his friends.

By now Bella had joined the others, standing alongside Adam and looking amazingly unconcerned. "Wind me up..." Bella hissed out the side of her mouth, as the menacing, although still very odd, strongman strode towards them.

"What?"

"Wind... me... up, quickly!" This time Bella gestured with her thumb back to the spot where her brass arm was locked into place just below her right shoulder. To his surprise, (although he was increasingly wondering why anything surprised him anymore), he saw a handle. Other than the fact it was stuck out of someone's back, it reminded him of the key used to wind the old clock that had taken pride of place on his mother's bedside table for years.

Hesitantly at first, then faster as the huge figure drew close, Adam turned the handle, which increasingly resisted his attempts to wind it tighter.

As he gave the handle one final turn, straining with both hands, the strongman reached them, raising his disproportionately large arms and grabbing towards Bella.

The look of triumph on his face disappeared completely a moment later as Bella's brass fist shot out lightning fast, grabbing a handful of his leotard. Despite his enormous size, and presumably comparably huge weight, Bella lifted him as easily as a bag of potatoes and then threw him across the ship's deck.

He slid to a halt against the feet of his, now very surprised looking, comrades, where he lay for a moment before pushing himself up onto his feet with a frustrated roar.

"Better give me a bit of space," Bella muttered under her breath, "I think I may have made him angry... or angrier."

This time the strongman came flying at them at full speed. Head down and furious, looking even more like a charging rhino as a result. Deciding very quickly to take Bella's advice Adam darted off to one side. Feeling helpless, painfully aware that trying a Daydream in the middle of the Sea of Dreams could easily overwhelm them all, he watched as Bella settled back into a relaxed looking crouch.

Watching from the side of the ship Adam cringed involuntarily as the strongman reached her, expecting to see her flying past him in moments. Instead, at the very last second, she dropped even lower. As she did, she also leant across to one side, which left only the rigid brass of her right arm in the path of her attacker.

There was an incredibly loud clanging sound and a moment later the strongman was flat on his back. From his position on the side-lines Adam could imagine small cartoon birds circling around the stunned man's head, feeling slightly disappointed when nothing so exciting happened. Instead, he just lay there groaning, winded and with the fight temporarily taken out of him.

From across the ship the two twins came flipping down towards them, reacting furiously to their companion's defeat. In the middle of the deck Bella was trying to re-adjust her arm, the impact having knocked it loose in its socket. Grimble was scrabbling inside his robes, dragging out a small glass vial of something that Adam expected was likely to go 'boom!', or perhaps cover their opponents in massive cobwebs or jelly – you could never really tell, and Lucid had grabbed a pole from the deck and had started to whirl it enthusiastically around his head.

Not really sure how he could help without the use of his Daydreams, Adam was running across to Bella to see if he could help re-attach her arm, when the whole increasingly surreal scene was interrupted by a booming shout.

"Enough! Pixie, Trixie stop."

The two tumbling acrobats paused immediately. One moment they were cartwheeling across the deck and the next they were stood side by side looking completely relaxed and slightly bored. One of the twins was closely inspecting the nails of her left hand, while the other had started to gaze out across the sea, hands on her hips and paying no attention to Adam or his friends whatsoever.

The tall man stepped forward, removing his top hat and giving a slight bow.

"It seems we have met our match on this occasion, and to be honest it is not exactly what we are most... comfortable doing. Allow me to introduce myself and my troupe. My name is Augustus Trimble, of the great Trimble Circus, although most just refer to me as the Ringmaster. No doubt you have heard of me."

Adam hadn't, although he wasn't really surprised by this, as there was much about Reverie he didn't know, especially outside the confines of the few cities he had visited during his time in the Dream World. From the looks on Lucid and his other companion's faces it seemed likely they hadn't either, although politeness, or more likely total confusion, prevented them from immediately saying so.

Not in the least perturbed Augustus continued. "No matter. My fame and that of my companions has perhaps been on the wane of late, which is why we now find ourselves in this rather unfortunate position." He turned his attention to the other odd characters that had invaded the Mayfly alongside him.

"These two are Pixie and Trixie, acrobats extraordinaire." One of the twins wiggled her fingers in a half-hearted wave, the other flipped onto one hand and blew the group a kiss with her other while balancing upside-down.

"Aggro is the strongman of our little collective." The Rhino man, still sprawled on the deck, managed to raise one hand in greeting with a slight groan.

"And this little fellow is Oomba," Augustus concluded, pointing to the crash helmet wearing Drömer. The wave he gave was the most enthusiastic by far, with the diminutive figure seeming genuinely pleased to meet them, despite their initially odd introduction.

Still unbalanced by the strange and sudden turn in events Adam struggled to think of a suitable response, so was relieved when Lucid stepped in.

"Pleased to meet you all I am sure. But in the circumstances, you can understand us feeling a little... cautious."

"What he means to say is you invade our ship, attack us and try to rob us. Which we don't like very much," glowered Grimble, still clutching a glass vial containing some offensive concoction or other and giving off the very strong impression he was still keen on using it.

"Understandable," the Ringmaster replied. "It was... rude to introduce ourselves in such a way, but desperate times have driven us to equally desperate actions. After our show was closed down we struggled to find any sort of work, despite our unique and undeniably fabulous skills."

As Augustus spoke, behind his bluster Adam could see and hear tell-tale signs of an underlying discomfort. His fingers were twisting the brim of the top hat he still grasped and while his voice remained deep and impressive, he sounded genuinely regretful.

"We tried every type of job... and we failed at them all. Finally, we found this ship and with the last remaining props and remnants from our show we started a new life on the seas. We have been pirates for... how long now?" he asked Oomba.

"About 3 months now," Oomba replied, after quickly consulting his fingers (counting them several times).

"And in that time, how many ships have we plundered?"

"Including this one?"

"Yes, including this."

Oomba checked his fingers once again, brow creased in concentration. Muttered few times under his breath and then re-checked his fingers one final time.

"None."

"Exactly," Augustus said, turning back to Adam. "It turns out that we are not really cut out for this line of work either. This was our first real chance to see how we fared living a life of adventure and piracy on the high seas and I think the general opinion is..."

"I don't really like it." Aggro rumbled from his prone position on the deck.

"Ditto," trilled Pixie,

"Likewise," added Trixie, still balancing upside down.

"By way of apology, perhaps we could offer you our hospitality this evening?" The Ringmaster said, replacing his top hat and gesturing back up at the larger vessel. "While we do not have much in the way of spoils, we did set out well-stocked with food and drink…"

Adam was about to turn the offer down, still unsure how much trust they could put in their strange visitors, when Augustus added, "…and we have seen things during our recent travels on the Dwam, things that it might help you to know."

Pricking up his ears at this Adam looked across to Lucid and the others. Even Grimble nodded, although without losing the grumpy look still plastered across his face.

CHAPTER 8

The circus troupe's vessel was just as oddly decorated on board as its unusual outward appearance had suggested. Adam and his friends were seated around a long table that had been dragged out onto the deck of the larger ship, now laden with a variety of tasty looking cakes, nibbles, and drinks. It had turned out that Oomba, when not busy trying to blow himself up, was a keen cook, and had spent the last hour enthusiastically bringing out plate after plate of food. Surrounding them, spread across the deck were a variety of rather sad looking circus props, adding an even more surreal atmosphere to the whole thing.

Off to one side of Adam was a small trampoline, which the twins had used while they were waiting for the food to put on a display of incredible mid-air acrobatics. To another side was a glass case containing a disturbingly life-like puppets head, with the sign hanging off the front promising that 'the Great Fernando' would tell your fortune for a few threads. Adam had resisted the brief temptation to try his luck, his previous experiences with fortune telling having been accurate but invariably filled with bad news. Just across from the table was a brightly painted and over-sized cannon, tethered securely to the deck, which Oomba had explained was how he had made his spectacular entrance earlier, using his experience as Reverie's only (surviving) Drömer cannonball.

Now that they were all settled around the table, with the circus troupe sat on one side and Adam and his friends on the other, the Ringmaster raised his glass in a toast.

"Welcome to our new home. While I feel that we may not perhaps be destined to succeed as pirates, we have lived on the Dwam for the last three months, a life we couldn't have imagined even a short while ago."

"During that time we have seen many things, some wonderful, and some... truly terrible," Augustus told them, his voice dropping slightly, encouraging his listeners to lean in. It was clear that he had something important to impart, but Adam also got the impression that there was some showmanship going on. Despite their change in circumstances, it seemed to Adam that their new hosts still enjoyed having an audience to perform to, and the Ringmaster was making the most of the story.

"You are only the second vessel we have come across in all of our time sailing this sea," Augustus continued.

"Which is one of the reasons why piracy is unlikely to be a viable long-term business," Oomba chimed in, "it's hard to be a pirate when there are no other ships."

"Yes, yes, thank-you Oomba," Augustus said, obviously a little annoyed that the atmosphere he'd carefully been creating had been punctured. "As I said, you are only the second ship we have come across..." he paused meaningfully and looked around the table.

"So, what was the first?" Lucid asked.

"Aha... seeing as you ask the question, obviously intrigued, then I shall tell you. The first was a ship like no other I have ever seen. It was just two nights ago, we feared we had sailed off course and drifted closer than we should to the land of Nightmares, when a huge vessel, even larger than our own came out of the mists." His voice dropped even lower as his tale continued. "There was no sound to be heard on board, no sign of life at all... at least not to begin with."

Despite himself, Adam found himself leaning in, fascinated to hear more. The slice of cake he had been about to tuck into remaining un-eaten, his hand paused half-way to his mouth.

"Something about that ship felt very wrong," Augustus told them. "It was to be our first attempt at piracy, but as it drew close we all somehow knew that to set even one foot on that ship would be the worst thing we could ever do. So instead we kept our heads down and did our best to pass it by without incident. Just as we were about to be clear of it we saw some movement on the deck, but nothing alive, instead there were shadows on that vessel... it was a ship of Nightmares."

Looking around the table Adam could see that the memory was still fresh with the rest of the troupe. Pixie and Trixie had both gone pale and even Aggro was looking a bit sick.

"I don't know exactly what they were, but they were like no Nightmares I had ever seen before," Augustus concluded with a theatrical shudder. "It was like they brought the night, patches of shadow surrounding them. I don't know why they let us pass without trouble."

"It was like they were looking for something," Aggro rumbled from across the table, "and I suppose that it wasn't us."

"But there's no one else out here, no one else sails the Sea of Dreams," Adam said. "No one else but...oh no..." he paused, a sensation like iced water running down his spine. "... no one else but us."

He sprang to his feet, "we have got to go!" he said, "if they were looking for us then you are all in danger. We have to go right now!"

Lucid, Grimble and Bella were already on their feet, their initial confusion quickly fading when they realised what Adam was saying. But as they started to make their way across the deck, politely declining Oomba's offer of further food, they were disturbed by a cry of alarm from one of the twins.

"Oh no, no, no... look!" Pixie shouted, as Trixie span on the spot to try and see what her sister was pointing at. Looking around, also following the line of her pointing finger, Adam spotted a swirling patch of shadow, still some way off, but more substantial looking than the regular mists that hung over the sea.

As it drew closer Adam could see that the shadow was billowing around the shape of another ship, even larger than the circus troupe's vessel. Even as it drew close the shape of the new arrival was hard to make out, still shrouded in shadows that seemed to cling to its sides, hiding any detail from Adam's gaze. Its sails hung limp, ragged and lifeless, yet it continued to approach them at speed, the hull creaking alarmingly as it neared them. Their dinner left and forgotten, chairs tipped and scattered in disarray, they all stared at the approaching ship, which was now heading directly for them.

"It's going to ram us, brace yourselves," the Ringmaster shouted, taking his own advice and wrapping his arms determinedly around the mast of his own vessel. The twin acrobats grabbed one arm each of Aggro, who had dropped into a crouch, looking as sturdy and immovable as a boulder. Adam and his friends also tried to prepare themselves and he spotted Augustus wince as Bella's brass hand scrunched deep into the wood of the nearest railing.

The next few seconds were a chaotic maelstrom of crashes, creaks, and bangs as the two vessels collided. Adam's world tipped onto its side as the deck of the circus ship bucked under his feet, feeling like his arm was going to be pulled from its socket as he gripped onto the ship's rail. For what felt like an infinitely long moment his feet left the deck and he hung in the air, suspended without gravity, splinters of fractured wood filling the air around him, several scratching his face on their way past, before reality came crashing back and he bumped painfully down onto the deck.

Looking around he could see his friends and the members of the circus crew slowly regaining their feet. Oomba was tapping the side of his crash helmet, and Lucid, having succeeded in staggering upright, was shaking his head looking confused and disoriented.

The larger vessel was now immediately alongside them, scraping roughly across the side of their ship, its deck several metres above their own. Adam and his companions all turned their gaze up, sharing the same uncomfortable premonition. All along the edge of the larger ship small shadowy figures appeared, shapeless at this distance, but radiating a sense of unmistakable cold menace. Adam could feel the heat of his pendant pulsing against his chest, warning him that Nightmares were close by, but he was also painfully aware that he couldn't react with a Daydream, even though every fibre of his being was shouting at him to do exactly that.

One after another the figures dropped from their vessel, down onto the deck in front of Adam and his friends. Each one landed with an unpleasant splash, like a lump of wet clay hitting a potter's wheel, before reforming into vaguely humanoid shapes.

While most of the companions had spent the last few moments in stunned inactivity, it seemed that Aggro was a firm believer in actions speaking louder than words. While the others were still trying to get their bearings, he bellowed angrily at the approaching shadowy forms before lowering his head and charging full tilt towards them, huge arms outstretched. Adam watched from the other side of the deck, waiting for the sound of impact as the strongman reached his target. But instead of the clash he was expecting there was an empty sucking sound as the closest shadow expanded slightly and appeared to completely swallow the charging figure. One moment he was there, the next there was just an empty space.

"You best leave my young friend," the Ringmaster shouted across, unwinding a long bullwhip as he spoke. To his right the acrobat twins were already darting between the shadowy shapes, flipping and vaulting across each other, always one step ahead of the Nightmares.

"What on earth is he doing?" Adam asked Grimble, unable to tear his eyes away, despite the increasingly urgent pull he could feel at his sleeve as Grimble tried to drag him away from the fight. "We need to stay... we need to help."

Augustus turned back to him. "This is our home," he said, "and this is my family... such as it is. We might not be cut out to be pirates, but the Dreamer made sure we all met out here for a reason, perhaps it was so we could see you safely on your way."

"You don't even know us," Adam pleaded, "you don't owe us anything."

"True enough," Augustus grunted back, "but I am going to venture that anyone who has Nightmares after them is probably on the side of good... at least you had better be young man. Now go, while you still have the chance."

On his other side, Oomba was muttering to himself, fiddling with the fuse hanging from the top of his crash helmet and a second, slightly shorter fuse on the brightly painted cannon. A couple of seconds later and Adam heard a low fizzing sound as he managed to light both. Giving Adam a quick salute he vaulted with surprising athleticism up into the yawning mouth of the cannon, which he had spun around to face down the deck towards the Nightmares.

"Come on," Adam heard Grimble say from just behind him. "We need to go, otherwise they're doing all of this for nothing." Adam was pretty sure he saw a small hand emerge from the end of the cannon, giving a 'thumbs up' and then there was a loud bang, which shook the deck, nearly knocking Adam off his feet. A small smouldering figure came flying out of the cannon's barrel, arms out to either side. Small fabric wings were stretched between his arms and his body, which seemed to give Oomba a tiny bit of control over his flight, while his crash helmet continued to fizz as the fuse burned down.

As he flew across the deck towards the advancing shadows Adam saw him tuck his arms into his body, and as he did his trajectory flattened and then dipped, diving towards the advancing shadowy shapes.

As they had when the strongman had charged at them the nearest shadow stretched wider, like the yawning mouth of some vast monster, and the flying, brightly coloured and violently fizzing figure vanished within it. Every eye on the ship focused on the spot where he had vanished, and then Adam heard a loud, but somehow incredibly distant, crumping explosion and a voice mutter "oh... bother." Then there was nothing but silence.

The tug on his arm got stronger and Adam turned to see Grimble staring up at him. "We have to go... now."

"But maybe I can do something, I could use a Daydream, just a small one?" Adam began.

"I know you want to, and I understand," Grimble told him, "but here on the Dwam you can't risk it. Even the smallest of Daydreams could end us all... and I see no way to stop those things."

He pulled again at Adam's sleeve, guiding him towards the gangplank back onto Bella's ship, where Bella and Lucid were already waiting for them. Several of the murky shapes had split from the main group and were now heading directly towards Adam, moving fast and purposefully and by the time Adam and Grimble had crossed the plank they were only a few metres away.

"Good luck to you," the Ringmaster shouted as he flicked his bullwhip towards them, the end wrapping itself around the plank. With a final flourish he jerked his arm back, the plank spinning into the air and crashing back amongst the massing shadows.

At either end of the Mayfly, Bella and Lucid had cut the ropes which tied the two ships together, and as the gangplank shattered on the deck of the circus ship they began to drift away. One of the shadowy shapes had been right on the edge of the ship as they pulled clear, and as a violent wave rocked both vessels it dropped into the swirling mists of the Dwam. As it touched the broiling surface the dark shadow twisted violently and then vanished, scattering in a cloud of rapidly dissipating dust.

The last that Adam saw of them the gymnast twins were still leaping and spinning amongst the increasingly dense shadows massing around them, while the Ringmaster roared his defiance, whirling the bullwhip around his head. Then the ship drew too far away for him to make out their figures amongst the gathering darkness.

CHAPTER 9

"What were those things?" Adam was stood by the wheel of the Mayfly, with Grimble on one side and Bella back in her usual relaxed slouch over the wheel on the other. Lucid had retired to the cabin, complaining of a bad headache, presumably caused by his earlier fall. Adam suspected that he was struggling with feelings of guilt, as they all were, having left the circus troupe to an unknown fate.

"I don't know." Grimble shrugged uncomfortably. Generally, it was hard to discern any emotion other than a general, underlying grouchiness behind his greying fur and scars, but this time his unease was written clearly across his face.

"I haven't ever seen anything like them before. The way that they just swallowed people up was…" Adam paused, unable to tear his mind away from the sight of Aggro and Oomba both disappearing into the strange shadowy void that the Nightmares had created.

"There was nothing we could do. Augustus and the others chose to stay and fight for their home, and to allow us to escape."

Adam nodded, although inside he still wondered if he could have done something more. The temptation to use his Daydreaming had been almost irresistible, despite the dangers of trying anything in the middle of the Dwam. Remembering their escape from the Nightmares when he had first discovered his abilities, and the way that Tremello and the other Sornette had fought off the fires while he escaped, Adam wondered how many more times others would put themselves in danger to help him. "No more," he promised himself. He couldn't face the thought of anyone else being put at risk because of him or his quest to find his mother. Next time the occasion demanded it he would stand and fight, regardless of consequence or personal risk.

That night as Adam tried to settle into his bunk, his attempts to sleep were constantly disturbed by images of the Nightmare vessel and the brave last stand of the circus folk. The realisation that he was leading his friends to the place the Nightmares called home and what that might mean finally sinking in. Eventually, it was only complete exhaustion that meant he was able to close his eyes and drift off, as the Mayfly gently rocked from side to side on the swell and sway of the Dwam as if it was trying its best to help him on his way.

CHAPTER 10

When Adam opened his eyes back in the Waking World they were heavier than usual, and getting out of bed much more of a challenge. The face that greeted Adam in the bathroom mirror obviously hated him, glaring back with bloodshot eyes that had large, dark bags under each one.

Charlie was already on his second round of breakfast when Adam finally joined him at the kitchen table. His normal, friendly morning greeting replaced with a mock gasp of horror when he turned around and saw Adam's face. "Yikes mate," he said, pretending to recoil and making a warding sign with his hands in Adam's direction. "No offence but you look like the zombie apocalypse has started and you're patient zero."

Adam's brain was still fuzzy with lack of genuine sleep, so he settled for a half-hearted zombie-like groan, stretching his arms out in front of him for a couple of seconds before letting them drop and slumping into the chair opposite Charlie.

"Wasn't a great night last night, to be honest," he told his friend. "Quite a lot happened, none of it very good, and I think people might have been hurt... or worse, because of me."

Charlies eyes widened in sympathy. "Don't worry mate," he said. "You don't need to talk about it now... unless you want to?"

Adam just shook his head and then let it fall into his hands, resting on the table.

"I'll get you some toast," Charlie muttered awkwardly, giving his friend a reassuring pat on the shoulder as he walked past. "Everything always seems better after toast."

As it turned out Charlie's powers of prediction were truly awful. Not only did Adam not feel any better after breakfast, which seemed to be resting unusually heavily in his stomach, but as the day went on fate seemed to be conspiring to add as many other problems and issues as it could. Walking to his form room, still groggy and not paying even his typically limited attention to his surroundings, he managed to bump into the back of one his classmates, knocking them into the open door of the locker they had been using with a painful sounding bump.

"Oh... I'm really sorry... I didn't mean..." Adam began. Then his heart sank even lower as he realised it was Nora he had clashed with, who turned, gave him a furious stare and then slammed the locker door shut before stomping off without a backward glance.

"Great," Adam muttered to himself, "Just great."

CHAPTER 11

Even though he knew that they were drawing close to the land of Nightmares, and that all sorts of unknown dangers were likely to be waiting for them, Adam felt an undeniable sense of relief when he re-joined his friends in Reverie that night. Once again, he woke in the middle of the Mayfly's deck, but this time his companions were fully occupied and didn't notice his arrival, instead they were clustered together at the far end of the ship, Bella pointing enthusiastically at something.

"What's going on?" Adam asked as he reached the rest, trying to spot whatever it was that had got everyone so excited.

Before anyone had a chance to answer him a sudden upheaval shook the Mayfly, tipping Adam off his feet. Grimble had also lost his footing, and judging from his muffled cursing, had landed rather heavily.

"It's her, the Deep Sleeper!" Bella shouted back, "she must have passed near the ship." As she spoke the deck tipped violently once again, although this time Adam had the foresight to grab tight to the ship's rails and he managed to stay standing.

Bella was almost erupting with obvious excitement. "I can't believe that we have run across her, the chances are tiny."

"Honestly, from experience, I am amazed that it's taken this long," Grimble growled as he got back to his feet, brushing himself down. "Every time I go anywhere with these two idiots if there is anything big or dangerous... or most often both anywhere nearby, that's where we end up."

"That's not completely true," Lucid said, giving Bella an apologetic grin.

"And if there isn't anything big and dangerous nearby," Grimble added, "then we just keep moving around until we do manage to find something... and then we prod it."

Adam was about to object to this too, but thinking back over his time in Reverie, he realised that Grimble maybe had a point, so decided to keep quiet.

Despite Grimble's pessimistic views, the remainder of the morning passed uneventfully. Bella had returned to the ship's wheel, although every now and then she would return to the ship's prow and stare longingly out into the mists of the Dwam, and Grimble had headed off to the cabin to put in some work on a diary of their travels that he had decided to start. "So that there's a surviving record of our journey when something terrible eats us all," was his typically reassuring reason.

Lucid had seated himself close to the back of the ship, creating a comfortable looking nest of sacking and coiled ropes that he was using as a giant beanbag. Although he felt slightly guilty about disturbing him, his fireside chat with Tremello had been playing on Adam's mind since the Grand Assembly. Although he had managed to pass across her good luck charm, there were still some big questions which had gone unanswered. It had taken him a while to get up the courage to find out anything more and now seemed like it could be a good chance to speak to Lucid without being disturbed by the others.

He didn't say anything to start with, instead finding a spot where he could sit alongside his friend in companionable silence, not really sure how to raise the subject. Eventually, he decided it would be easier to just bite the bullet and say exactly what was on his mind.

"Do you ever miss life on the Weave?" he tried as an opening, seeing how comfortable Lucid looked, relaxing on deck.

"A little," Lucid replied from under the brim of his hat, which was tilted forward covering his eyes. "In some ways, this reminds me of those times, despite everything I have slept better in that little cabin than I ever do back in Nocturne, it must be the movement of the ship."

"Do you ever think about going back?"

"No... not anymore," Lucid said, after a pause which was just long enough to feel slightly uncomfortable. When he spoke again there was a sombre depth to his voice that suggested his words were coming from a time or place long past. "Once upon a time maybe, but too many things have happened, I have journeyed much too far."

Adam realised that now, if ever, would be his chance to find out what it was that kept Lucid separate from the rest of his people, and steeled himself.

"What was it... what happened when you came to Nocturne?" he asked, the words tripping over themselves in his hurry to get them all out before he lost his nerve. "Whatever it was Tremello and the others miss you... Tremello especially I think."

Lucid's hat was still over his eyes, so it was impossible to read his emotions, but Adam thought he could see a slight flush of colour on his cheeks. When he spoke again it wasn't a direct answer to Adam's question.

"I have heard about a creature in your world," he began, "that lives in a shell all of its life, deep in your oceans. Occasionally something small and painful, like a piece of grit, gets inside that shell and the creature protects itself by wrapping that painful little intruder in layer after layer until that piece of grit is completely covered."

Adam nodded, although Lucid couldn't see him. He was pretty sure he could remember a biology lesson where they had been taught about how pearls were formed, something beautiful and valuable created from a fragment of unwanted dirt.

"It takes a long time, or so I am told," Lucid continued, "until eventually there is nothing to see but a smooth, shining treasure. But somewhere, deep and unseen within it, that original little piece of grit, the irritant that caused it all, is still there right in the centre... and it always will be."

Adam waited to see if Lucid was going to explain any further, but it seemed that was all he was willing to share, leaving Adam to interpret the meaning of his words as well as he was able.

He was settling back, turning the discussion over in his mind, when he was disturbed by a sudden jolt, the deck of the Mayfly jumping underneath him and tipping him off the crate he had been using as a makeshift seat. By the time he got back onto his feet Lucid was also standing, his top hat now perched back on top of his head.

"Come on," Lucid said, and he led the way back to the wheel, where Bella was waiting, joined shortly after by Grimble, who looked like he had just woken up. Where the sky had previously been still and clear there were now dark clouds, and a strong wind was whipping noisily across the deck.

"That's impossible," said Adam, "it was sunny just a few seconds ago, a storm can't start that quickly... can it?"

"It's a sign that she's back," Bella told them excitedly. "It's the Deep Sleeper. Wait here, I need to get something." As she spoke the ship rocked violently again, although Adam saved himself from another fall by grabbing onto the wheel.

Meanwhile, Bella had made her way across to the central mast and was busily rummaging amongst the various odd attachments hanging from it. "Here," Bella shouted across to Adam and his companions, her voice straining to carry above the roar of the wind, "grab hold of these and tie yourself to it." A line snaked its way across the deck, skittering to a halt by Adam's feet. Rather than being a rope, as Adam had expected, it looked to be an odd composite, metal and fabric inter-twined into a hybrid that seemed both stronger and more flexible than either of its parts. With a couple of well-practiced throws, Bella heaved matching lines to Grimble and Lucid who set about strapping themselves into the lightweight harnesses at the end of each line.

The boat bucked again as another swell in the Dwam caught them, unbalancing Adam who slid across the deck away from the security of his harness. The deck had tilted so far that he wasn't sure he was going to be able to stop himself. All he could see were the railings at the edge of the deck getting rapidly closer to his feet, which were scrabbling ineffectually against the slippery planks. At the last moment, he managed to wrap his arms around one of the sturdy posts that Bella used when tying the ship in to dock. His arm felt like it was going to be wrenched out of its socket, but it was still better than plummeting into the swirling mists of the Dwam, so gritting his teeth he hung on through the pain. After a further agonizing moment, the ship righted itself and Adam was able to drag himself back across to the strange harness and pull the straps over his shoulders. Bella and the others had apparently had more success and were already wearing theirs, although Grimble looked far from happy.

"Bit of a hairy moment," Lucid said, nodding in Adam's direction.

"I'm fine, it was nothing," Adam managed, with more conviction than he really felt. Now that the adrenaline of the moment had passed his legs suddenly felt like they were made of jelly and it was all he could do just to keep standing, pretending that he hadn't just been completely terrified.

"Don't think for a minute that this means I intend going anywhere off this ship," Grimble growled as he tried to re-arrange his clothes. "Especially if there is a giant beasty of some kind swimming around underneath us." He stopped his grumbling for a moment to have another go at adjusting the harness, which was bunching his robes uncomfortably around his waist. The sight of this, even in their current predicament, was making the corner of Lucid's mouth twitch with the beginnings of a grin.

"You should take these as well," Bella yelled, passing out a small brass cylinder to each of them. If you do get knocked overboard, your lines will tether you back to the ship, but I wouldn't recommend breathing in the mists of the Dwam. If the worst comes to the worst, use these." She mimed putting the tube, width-wise, into her mouth.

Grimble was turning his cylinder over in his hands, a look of grudging admiration on his face.

"A breathing tube, pretty clever," he shouted over the wind, which had picked up and was now blowing across the Mayfly, tumbling empty crates and tugging scraps of material taut. "How long do they last?"

"You should have about 5 minutes, maybe a little longer if you don't breathe too hard."

"Let's just hope we don't need to use them," Lucid said, with what turned out to be completely misguided optimism and terrible timing. As he finished speaking the biggest upheaval yet hit the ship, almost flipping it onto its side. Adam's viewpoint twisted with it, suddenly finding the deck gone from underfoot. For a second everything seemed to be caught in a freezeframe. Lucid had his long limbs outstretched, reaching wildly for the security of the mast, just out of his reach. Grimble was dangling on the end of his safety line, his eyes firmly shut and his arms rigid by his side, looking for all the world like an incredibly grumpy yo-yo. Finally, Bella was still grimly holding onto the wheel of the Mayfly, the incredible strength of her brass right arm somehow managing to maintain its grasp, although her legs were flailing out behind her.

Then time caught up with them all and Adam was over the side of the ship, rapidly sinking through the churning mists of the Dwam. There was almost no change in atmosphere as he tumbled down, just a loss of vision, his sight suddenly clouded. He gave an automatic, gasping inhalation of breath and immediately wished he hadn't. Although the mist had provided almost no resistance to his descent, it felt immediately heavy and painful in his lungs, making him gag and cough.

Trying to fight down feelings of panic, Adam held his breath, biting down on the further coughs that were trying to escape. He could also feel an uncomfortable sharpness digging into his right palm and realised that he was still gripping the breathing tube that Bella had given him. Hoping that he had remembered what she had shown him, he jammed it into his mouth, inhaling sharply.

A moment later his descent was suddenly and uncomfortably halted as the safety line jerked him to an abrupt stop, nearly making him spit the tube out again, as the harness tightened across his chest and stomach.

Dangling like a lure on a fishing line, a comparison that he didn't feel very comfortable with, Adam tried to get his bearings, looking around trying to see... anything. Unfortunately, all that he could see was swirling mist in every direction. He remembered Grimble's warnings that the Weave, and presumably the Dwam, had no known bottom, that you would fall forever. Subconsciously he gripped the line that secured him to the Mayfly even more tightly, wondering:

1. What had happened to the others;
2. Which way was up;
3. Whether the Deep Sleeper was likely to eat people.

The last thought in particular was weighing heavily on his mind and was quickly joined by an additional worry. He was pretty sure that Bella had said the breathing tubes only lasted for five minutes and he had no idea how much time had already passed. Remembering what she had told them, he tried to calm his breathing, making the fresh air he could feel filtering slowly from the tube last as long as possible.

Unsure what else to do he gripped the line, which he hoped still tethered him to the Mayfly and the surface of the Dwam, and started to climb, hand over hand. After the chaos of the surface, it was eerily silent and surprisingly still, the movement of the deeper mists muted and gentle compared to the crashing waves above, although unfortunately the lower depths of the Dwam also provided almost no buoyancy, and as a result the climb was exhausting. Every now and then he would catch a flicker of light or glimmer of an image glowing for a moment, as if an unseen projector was casting a picture onto a shifting canvas and he remembered that, just like the Weave, the Dwam was made of dreams, past and present.

To his right, an image of a young boy, playing with a train set shimmered for a moment, before drifting away and out of sight. Directly in front of him, there was an elderly woman sat drinking a cup of tea with a friend, both laughing silently at some shared, unheard joke, before this too dissipated as the mists parted, and to his left was the pupil of an enormous, unblinking eye.

Adam blinked, the eye was still there and looked considerably more solid and substantial than the other visions. Gulping, Adam twisted his body around to face the eye fully. It was nearly as large as Adam's entire body, and now it was so near he could see the heavy folds of skin around its edges, emerging from the mists.

"That's definitely not a dream," Adam gulped to himself, trying not to swallow the breathing tube in his panic. The massive eye was now right by him, with an equally vast pupil in its centre staring right at Adam. As he looked back into the inky blackness he could feel his panic slowly fading away, replaced instead by a feeling of incredible calmness and peace. The vast creature by his side, which Adam assumed could only be the Deep Sleeper that Bella had spoken of, continued to get closer, until finally it nudged gently against him.

Its body was huge, stretching off so far into the distance that Adam couldn't see where it ended. It reminded him of a Whale, but on a much, much larger scale, its skin pale and deeply ridged with age.

His attention was caught by a glistening cluster of gem-like stones, which seemed to be embedded into the creature's body. Without fully understanding why, Adam felt his hand reaching out to grasp the cluster without any particular prompt from his brain. As his fingers closed around the gems his mind was almost immediately overwhelmed by a bombardment of mental images, cycling through his brain one after another, too fast to really comprehend.

There were dreams he recognised as his own, fragments of fondly remembered stories with his mother, and snatches of more recent memories. The battle with Isenbard and the Horror, the showdown with Chimera and the farewell to Mittens, all passing through his mind so quickly he struggled to make sense of one before the next began.

After these more familiar memories, a series of images that he didn't recognise danced in front of his eyes. The first of these was Bella, one of her eyes glowing fiercely with a mysterious light, next was a vast cavern, heavy with unexplained menace. Then a far more pleasant looking scene took its place, a carpet of green grass dotted with vibrantly coloured flowers spreading out into the distance. Finally, this vision faded too, replaced with one last scene in which Adam couldn't see much at all, just the rush of air passing his face accompanied by the feeling of flight and an underlying sense of fear, of fleeing from something... something huge, angry and terrifying.

When his mind cleared the first thing Adam noticed was that the breathing tube was no longer in his mouth, which was not the most promising start. He blinked rapidly, while also trying not to breathe in. He hurt all over, his back was aching, and he could feel a prodding pain halfway between his shoulder blades. A blurry shape appeared in front of his face, slowly resolving itself into a very welcome sight.

"Lucid!" Adam coughed in relief. "What... where?" As he spoke, he realised that the pain in his back was caused, at least partly, by the fact that he was leaning against a pile of rough wooden crates. Rough, but wonderfully, reassuringly, solid.

Lucid's expression of concerned relief changed to one of wonderment.

"One minute you were gone, somewhere deep within the Dwam, we were trying to pull you up and then your rescue line went slack."

Adam looked down at himself as Lucid continued his explanation. The harness that had secured him to the rescue line was completely gone, no sign of it remaining.

"Then there was a sudden, final wave that washed over the deck and when it had gone all that was left behind was... you."

The last few frenetic moments of his time under the Dwam were starting to resurface in Adam's mind. The huge staring eye of the Deep Sleeper, the strange visions he had experienced, and the feeling of the cluster of glowing crystallised dreams, gripped tightly in his hand.

With this last memory fresh in his mind Adam looked down at his right hand, which was still clenched by his side and slowly opened his fingers. There, balanced on his palm, glowing gently like a new moon, was a small, perfectly round crystal. Off to one side, he heard Bella give an involuntary gasp.

Gem still grasped firmly, Adam pushed himself up into a standing position. He still felt woozy and had to lean against the crates once he had regained his feet, but in the circumstances, he wasn't about to complain.

His companions were stood in a rough semi-circle around him, a mixture of very different expressions on their faces. Lucid was still looking bemused, while Grimble was grimacing, but slightly less than normal, which Adam took as a sign he must be feeling incredibly relieved by Adam's safe return. But of all of them, it was Bella's face that told the most involved story.

In the short time he had known her, other than the brief moments when she had spoken of her love of adventure and her travels on the Dwam, Adam was used to Bella looking out at the world with a mixture of dark humour and disdain. She had always given him the impression of someone who had been rather disappointed by life and who had set her expectations accordingly. Without her mouth twisted into its normal cynical smile she looked very different, younger and with a yearning look written clearly across her face. A look that he realised he couldn't ignore.

Taking a final look down at the glowing crystal still grasped in his right hand he reached out and offered it to her.

"I think you should probably have this," he said, a little shyly, but increasingly sure of his decision as he spoke. "I'm not sure why, but I think that it was supposed to be for you, not me."

Bella slowly dropped her gaze down to the glimmering sphere, reaching out towards it with a tentative, unsure hand.

"Are you sure?" she managed to say, her voice quiet but clear, the raging winds of earlier having completely dropped away, leaving the air around them still and silent. "What you have there could be one of the rarest things ever found in our world."

Adam nodded. "I'm certain," he said, and he was, surprisingly so. The visions he had experienced as he clung to the side of the Deep Sleeper had felt incredibly real, and he could still clearly recall the sight of Bella, her eye shining with an impossible light. "The Deep Sleeper wanted you to have this."

Gingerly Bella plucked the orb from Adam's outstretched palm and held it out in front of her, looking at it from every angle with childlike rapture.

"It's beautiful," she finally said softly. "Everything I thought it would be."

Still holding the crystal gingerly, she left the rest of the group, heading off to the small cabin at the back of the ship. "I won't be long," she told them, pulling the door closed behind her.

When she emerged a few minutes later she was wearing an eye patch, covering the socket where her glass eye generally sat, glowering out at the world. Her broad smile told a story all of its own, which was reinforced by the new lightness in her uneven stride as she re-joined them. She looked both younger and more enthusiastic than Adam could remember, glowing with an inner happiness which was a world away from her normal cynicism.

"So?" Adam asked.

Bella didn't answer. Instead, with her grin broadening even further, she lifted the eyepatch gently. As she did a warm glow spilled out, brightening as more of her eye socket was revealed. There sat snuggly in the place previously occupied by her glass eye was the shining, spherical crystal that Adam had given her.

CHAPTER 12

When Adam awoke back in Charlie's spare room, the memory of Bella's new glowing eye was still fresh in his mind, and for the first time in a while he felt that things were going his way, so much so that he decided that today would be the day he would finally sort things out with Nora. Charlie had an early dentist appointment with his parents, so this time Adam went around to Nora's house alone.

By the time he got there some of his earlier optimism had started to drain away, his finger pausing half-way to her doorbell as a nagging voice inside his head suggested this wasn't the best idea after all. Ignoring the persistent doubt, Adam pressed on the doorbell particularly hard, trying to prove a point to his more indecisive self. Still, when the door swung slowly open, he had the unpleasant combination of a dry mouth and damp hands.

Rather than Nora opening the door, as he had hoped, it was her mum. She looked a lot like Nora, but with lighter hair and glasses, and on the few previous occasions they had briefly met Adam had always got the impression that she didn't really approve of him. The look she gave him now didn't do much to change that view, apparently disappointed that it was him at the door rather than someone more appealing, like a door-to-door salesman... or a plague of rats.

"Um... morning Mrs. Penworthy," Adam began, trying his most winning smile, which had about as much effect as flicking a charging bull with a small, damp, flannel. "Is Nora in?"

"Sorry Adam," Nora's mum replied, although she didn't look particularly sorry. "You just missed her. She wanted to get down to the Library as soon as it opened."

After a hurried goodbye, which wasn't returned, Adam decided to head for the Library himself. He didn't feel quite ready to give up and meeting somewhere neutral might even make things easier, with Nora less likely to fly off the handle quite so loudly.

As normal the old building was almost completely deserted, with only the Head Librarian and two old ladies, who seemed to live pretty much permanently on the worn sofas in the fiction section, occupying the ground floor. The Council had tried running special events over the last few weeks to increase the number of people using the Library, including a coffee morning, but this had just resulted in the two ancient regulars drinking multiple coffees, getting rather giddy and scaring off the one new potential visitor that the event had attracted.

Not finding her downstairs, Adam presumed that Nora would be up on the first floor in the reference section, so headed straight up, trying not to make eye contact with the two old ladies. While very pleasant, (when not over-caffeinated), he knew that once he had been caught in conversation with them he may as well give up on any further plans for his day.

Sure enough, Nora was sat at one of the desks on the first floor, apparently deeply engrossed in research, head bowed over a textbook. Seeing her sat there on her own filled Adam with regret, a far cry from the happier memories the place held for him. The Library had been, for a while at least, the place where he, Charlie and Nora would escape to. Somewhere they could meet, fairly certain that they wouldn't be disturbed, and talk about the latest happenings in Reverie.

There wasn't really any need to come here at all. They all had the internet at home and access to pretty much anything they needed for schoolwork, but it had become a haven for the three of them. Even though it seemed that Nora was no longer able to join him in the Dream World, it looked like she still treated the Library as somewhere she could escape to.

He quickly ran through a few greetings in his head, trying to think of a reason he could give for accidentally bumping into her. Unfortunately, he was so deep in thought that he failed to navigate his way around the nearest chair, clattering it with his leg and making her look up in surprise at the noise.

"Um, hi Nora," Adam managed, rubbing his bruised shin and trying not to wince. Not exactly the casual opening he had intended.

The look she gave him was less friendly than he'd hoped. He knew that she was struggling with being unable to re-enter Reverie and despite the fact that it wasn't his fault, he still felt guilty about the ease with which he flipped between the two worlds. He had pretty much stopped sharing his tales of the Dream World with her, or with Charlie when she was around, as the stories just increased her frustration at not being able to join him there.

It had been going on for a few weeks now, and the increasingly frosty way that she spoke to him had been getting too much to bear, especially after how much they had been through together. Despite this not being the opening he had hoped for, he felt some of the optimism from earlier in the day return. He was going to have things out with Nora, talk everything through and try and mend the cracks in their friendship before they grew too big to fill.

"What do you want?" she asked, sounding tired and grumpy.

Without waiting for an invitation Adam plonked himself down in the chair opposite her.

"I wanted to see you," he replied. "We haven't talked in a bit and... I missed chatting with you."

"Fine, what do you want to talk about... that's not to do with Reverie, dreams or nightmares... or adventures generally, because I am not interested in talking about any of those things."

Adam thought quickly, he had intended to talk about exactly that, or more specifically about the problems that Nora was having with entering Reverie and how that shouldn't affect them being friends in the Waking World. All of his carefully planned words went straight out of his head, along with the reconciliation he had imagined when the day had begun.

His confusion must have been pretty clear as, after a few moments of awkward silence, Nora sighed.

"You see... we don't have anything else to talk about. It was only Reverie that we had in common." She slammed her textbook closed and stuffed it into her bag. "And now we don't have that."

Without saying anything further, she pushed her chair back and stomped off, leaving Adam sat open-mouthed, still unable to find the right words to call her back. He was still sitting there five minutes later when he finally realised what he should have said.

His walk home was far less optimistic than his walk to the Library had been. Footsteps that had felt light on the way there were ponderous, his shoulders slumped rather than upright. "Why does it all have to be so tricky?" Adam thought to himself, staring down at the pavement and kicking a small stone unfortunate enough to be in his way hard enough to skitter it halfway across the road.

His mood hadn't improved at all by the time he got back to Charlie's house, which led to a particularly awkward dinner with the family. Charlie was unable to talk or eat properly, his mouth still numb after getting a filling at the dentists and Adam wasn't in the mood to fill the silence as he normally would have done. He ended up going to bed far earlier than he needed to, and long before he was able to sleep.

Laying there, thinking back over the failures of the day, he found himself wishing for the first time in a long time that his life could return to being normal.

CHAPTER 13

When Adam next awoke in Reverie it was immediately clear that this passing wish was not going to come true any time soon. Finding himself back on the deck of the Mayfly, balanced on the edge of the vast sea of dreams, the knowledge that he was about as far from a normal life as it was possible to be came crashing back. It also seemed that things had moved on since his last visit. Rather than standing in her normal slouched position, Bella was standing bolt upright with a worried look on her face.

"You've arrived at an opportune time," Lucid told him, in response to Adam's quizzical look in Bella's direction. "It looks like we are near to the end of our journey, but unfortunately our arrival isn't going as smoothly as we might have hoped."

Ahead of them, Adam could see the first glimpses of a dark and rocky coastline emerging from the mists of the Dwam, a coastline that seemed to be getting closer alarmingly quickly.

"Land... or at least something similar to land... ahoy," Bella shouted across the deck. "I would grab hold of something... we are caught in a current that will take us right into that bay, much... much too fast."

Grimble gave a resigned sigh and wrapped his short arms as far around the mast as they could reach, making up for what they lacked in length with a combination of natural strength and extreme stubbornness. "It seems like every single day we get to fall off this thing," he grumbled, "we might as well have swum here."

"Your welcome to try that on the way back," Bella snapped, staring intently at the fast-approaching rocky outcrops that guarded the entrance to the bay. "But for the moment, hold on tight... and shut up!"

Lucid had wrapped his arm through one of the ropes tethered to the outside walls of the cabin and was doing his best to brace himself, which left Adam as the only one still needing to find a secure spot. Determined that he wasn't going to spend any more time in the Dwam, and thinking he had probably used up his luck in that respect in any event, Adam copied Lucid and shoved both forearms through the rope just behind his friend, gripping tightly with both hands.

The ship fell silent as the companions all focused on the land in front of them, which was now only seconds away. Despite the speed of their approach, and the roughness of the mists, Bella had managed to steer the Mayfly through the clusters of rocks which poked fang-like from the Dwam without harm. Adam could see the concentration creasing her brow as she gripped the wheel and felt another surge of admiration for her obvious skill, although this was quickly replaced by a combination of anxiety and sheer, blind panic.

When they were about five hundred metres from land Bella reached down from the wheel with one hand and pulled on a small brass lever. There was a loud clicking sound as some hidden mechanism was triggered and two long arms pivoted up from either side of the mast, with an expanse of material stretched tautly between them, much larger, but shallower than the mainsail that Adam was used to seeing.

The wind was against them and as the material snapped tight it acted as a giant air-brake, jolting Adam's arms uncomfortably against the resistance of the ropes still wrapped securely around them as the Mayfly suddenly slowed.

Despite this, the speed of their approach to the land of the Nightmares remained uncomfortably fast. The Dwam was swelling and rolling under the Mayfly as it grew shallower, the misty waves crashing against the shelves of dark rock directly ahead of them.

There was an unpleasant scraping, rasping sound, as the Mayfly's hull started to drag, and then a violent shudder as their progress suddenly slowed even further, throwing them all forward. Because Adam's arms were still firmly entangled in the ropes tethering him to the ship, rather than being tossed across the deck, he was swung around, pivoting around face first towards the mast. The last thing he heard was Bella shouting a final warning and a terrible splintering sound. Then his head made contact with the solid wood of the mast and everything went black.

Shooting upright in his bed, Adam clutched his head with a groan. "Well, that probably has to be the record for the shortest time I've managed to stay in Reverie."

It was still pitch black in Charlie's spare room, the red LED numbers of the bedside clock blinking out the time at just after eleven-o-clock. Sighing to himself Adam tried to disentangle himself from his bedclothes, his arm having got wrapped fairly tightly in his sheet, he presumed as an unconscious replica of his last memory in Reverie, twisting the ropes of the Mayfly around himself.

Experience had taught him that getting immediately back to sleep wasn't going to happen, so instead Adam grabbed a book from the bedside table, clicked on the lamp and settled down to read for a while, hoping that he would naturally feel sleepy again as soon as possible.

The book turned out to be surprisingly gripping, and in other circumstances Adam would have happily kept reading chapter after chapter, just to find out what happened next. But tonight he had far more important things to do, so he decided to leave the story and try something less interesting and more likely to encourage sleep. Looking around the room his gaze settled on his revision notes for the maths exam, an unwelcome reminder that there were evil things in this world too.

The notes did however have the desired effect, and while he didn't manage to learn or remember anything useful, within a few minutes his eyes were heavy with a combination of renewed tiredness and randomised mathematical despair. Before much longer his head dropped into his chest, the notes still cradled on his lap, and he jerked back awake in Reverie. But this time he awoke with the feeling of hard rock under his back, rather than the wooden deck of the Mayfly.

Overhead the sky was a deep red, with no sign of the mists that had been a constant companion during their travels across the sea of dreams. Immediately in front of him was a tall cluster of dark, volcanic looking rocks, behind which Lucid and Grimble were both sheltering.

"Thank goodness you're back," Lucid said, reaching down and helping Adam to his feet. "Things have been a bit... tricky for the last couple of hours." Adam looked around, trying to get his bearings.

"Where's Bella?"

"Still with the Mayfly," Lucid replied. "Trying her best to find a way to re-float it if she can."

"It took some serious bumps when we hit the shore," Grimble told him. "But whatever shortcomings that dodgy shipwright had, he seemed to know his business. The Mayfly was still in one piece, more or less, when we left."

"Since then we have been moving inland, trying to find out exactly where we've landed," Lucid added. "But it has been extremely slow. This place is crawling with Nightmares, and not ones chasing after their dreamer like we have seen before. These are just wandering freely... and there are a lot of them."

Grimble scowled across at his taller friend. "A few times we have been this close to being seen," he said, holding two stubby fingers a fraction of an inch apart. "Some people rather stand out, what with their stupidly tall hat sticking out above the rocks."

Lucid huffed and lifted a hand to touch the brim of his top hat protectively. "I told you, I am not leaving my hat."

"Anyway," Grimble said. "We need to find an alternative to all this skulking between piles of rocks. Sooner or later we are going to run out of luck... or run into a Nightmare who isn't so dumb as to think it's normal to have a massive hat sticking out from behind the nearest boulder."

"We could try over there," Adam said, pointing at a spot on the horizon where the scrubby wasteland gave way to something more impressive, the peak of a low mountain rising above its surroundings. "I don't know if there is anything that way, but it's the only thing I can see anywhere near, and maybe if we climb up it a bit, we could get a better view."

"Why don't you just fly up and look around?" Lucid asked, "I think we're far enough away from the Dwam now that you could try it without anything too bad happening."

Grimble gave a particularly exasperated sigh. "We have just about got away with Nightmares seeing your hat and not raising the alarm. I am pretty sure we would find it hard to explain away a flying child!"

"Fine," Lucid replied, and without a further word to his two companions struck out towards the distant mountain, one hand still clutching his hat protectively.

"Fine," Grimble growled and stomped off in the same general direction.

Sighing to himself and wishing that he had been knocked unconscious for longer, rather than having to deal with the squabbling of his two friends, Adam trudged after them.

The mountain turned out to be much bigger, but also much further away than it had initially looked. By the time the three of them reached its base most of the day had gone and the sky was beginning to darken. Although he didn't have any particular reason for thinking it, Adam was feeling increasingly certain that being out when nightfall came in the land of Nightmares might be a bad idea.

Up close the mountain was formed of the same dark rock that seemed to make up much of the land that Adam had seen so far. It reminded him of cooled lava, rippled and slightly unnatural looking. Around the base there were clusters of smaller rocky outcrops, although he was yet to see any sign of plant life, and then, maybe fifty metres to the right he spotted something that caught his attention.

"Look," he gestured to the other two, "over there."

Following his pointing finger Lucid and Grimble stared across at a spot that could have been easily mistaken at this distance as a patch of darker shadow, but looking more closely the light fell differently, sucked away into an opening of some kind.

As they got closer they had to pause, staying hidden while a pack of roaming Nightmares ambled past. Adam could just make out the growled conversation between the two nearest monsters.

"So... you on guard duty again today?"

"Uuugh... hate guard duty, I'm supposed to be off giving nightmares to an estate agent, whatever one of those is, pretending that I'm a well appointed, centrally located flat. But every time she gets close to selling me it turns out that I've got terrible problems with damp."

"Har..Har.." his companion replied, "sounds about right to me."

"Shut up..." the first Nightmare grumbled, jabbing his companion in the ribs with one giant, bony elbow as they disappeared off into the distance.

With the danger past, Adam turned his attention back to the opening in the rockface.

"What do you think?" he asked. "Shall we have a look inside?"

"Well it's a dark, sinister-looking cave in the middle of a horrible barren wasteland filled with the worst imaginable Nightmares," Grimble replied, looking particularly unhappy about the situation, "what could possibly go wrong?"

"Not many other options at the moment," Lucid added, slightly more optimistically. "It will be night here soon, and hopefully whatever is in that cave will be no worse than spending the night outside."

"Fine…" Grimble conceded grumpily, although he made them wait impatiently for a couple of minutes while he made another entry in his journal. Presumably something along the lines of, 'followed two idiots into a cave containing certain death.'

It took one quick dash to reach the cave entrance and then the three of them were inside, the gathering dusk of the wasteland giving way to the much thicker darkness within the cave itself. The walls were made of the same unpleasant looking rock as the rest of the wasteland, uneven and looking slightly melted, gathered more thickly closer to the ground. Ridged and grey like the loose skin of an elephant.

"How far does this go?" Lucid muttered.

Grimble reached into an inside pocket and pulled out a small glass vial which he shook violently. There was a gentle fizzing sound and the liquid within the vial began to glow, at first gently and then increasingly brightly, until the shadows of Adam and his companions danced across the walls.

"Let's find out."

They had been walking for about ten minutes when they first heard it, a dull, repetitive thudding sound that vibrated up through Adam's legs. He unconsciously started to count the seconds between each thud, which became increasingly loud the deeper into the cave they walked. Thirty seconds, then a thud, then another forty before the next, then forty-five, then thirty again. The same pattern was repeated over and over, slightly varying gaps between the reverberating sounds as Adam and his friends continued to make their way down the uneven corridor.

After a few more minutes, during which time the sounds had become much louder, the vibrations making Adam's teeth shake, the tunnel gradually widened with a much brighter glow bleeding down towards them. The sight that met Adam as they reached the end of the tunnel felt oddly familiar, although he was sure he had never seen it before.

Rather than the previously cramped confines of the tunnels, the space opened up into a huge cavern, so large that Adam struggled to see the opposite side. The source of the strange, rhythmic pounding noise was immediately obvious. Right in the centre of the cave was a giant metal frame, nearly a hundred metres high. Within it was a massive shard of rock, shaped to fit the interior of the frame and connected to huge chains which ran up to its top, creating a gigantic pulley system.

All around this were several hundred unkempt looking workers, emaciated and grubby, dozens pulling on each of the chains. After thirty seconds or so of strenuous heaving, slowly inching the stone pillar higher and higher within the frame, there was a rumbling drum-beat. As the drum struck the workers released the chains and the pillar plummeted into the ground, the resulting impact reverberating across the cavern. A few seconds passed, the drum struck again, and inch by painful looking inch the whole process started again.

A series of long open crevices centred around the base of the strange construct ran across the floor of the cave, and with every impact the cracks widened ever so slightly. Along each one of those cracks, dozens more of the miners worked ceaselessly, chipping away at the open rock-faces and levering wedges of dark rock out and onto trolleys, where yet more workers broke these down into smaller and smaller pieces.

Every now and then one of the miners would give a shout and raise their arm, holding chunks of rock no bigger than their fist into the air. When they did a Nightmare would shamble over, take the rock from them and carry it off towards a raised platform at the far end of the cavern. The only other opening that Adam could see was directly below this platform.

"Looks like that's where we need to go next," Lucid said.

"How do we know this is even the right direction?" Grimble asked. "For all we know we are just heading deeper and deeper into somewhere we don't want, or need, to be."

"I know it sounds weird," Adam told him, still focusing on the tunnel entrance on the other side of the cavern, "but I have a really strong feeling that we are going the right way." He pushed himself back off the wall, willing himself to stay positive, despite how tired he was feeling. "All I know is that my mum is near... somewhere," he said. "I don't know how I know that, but I am sure of it. The closer we get to the centre of this place, the closer I feel she is."

Lucid gave a short laugh. "Sounds just like your mother," he replied. "She's a lot like you in that respect. If there is some sort of terrible danger, horrible calamity or imminent disaster you seem to be drawn almost helplessly towards it. Must be some sort of genetic predisposition towards making really awful choices that has been passed down, mother to son."

He clapped Adam on the back reassuringly. "Come on then, let's find your mum, get out of this place and leave Grimble behind."

"Oh, very nice," Grimble grumbled to himself, as they began to work their way slowly across the cavern, jinking from rocky outcrop to outcrop, doing their best to stay out of sight. "I am sure that whoever runs this place is lovely, if we're really lucky we might even get to meet them."

As they took shelter behind a pile of rubble close to one of the areas where workers were breaking down the larger chunks of rock Adam had his first chance to get a better look at them. In addition to looking hungry, tired and miserable, most also had lengths of chain shackling their legs together. "They're not miners... they're slaves." Adam muttered to himself.

"Ullo Mr. Lucid," rumbled a deep, familiar voice from directly behind where Adam and his friends were crouched. Adam span on the spot, nearly twisting his ankle, and looking behind him saw an unmistakably large and looming figure he recognised from their brief meeting back in Nocturne.

"Carter," said Lucid, voice filled with surprise. "What on earth are you... I mean how..." he slowly wound down into confused silence, the look of shock on his face so comical that in other, less horrible circumstances, Adam was pretty sure he would have laughed by now.

"Bit strange to say the least Mr. Lucid," Carter said, wiping one massive fist across his forehead, leaving a dark, grubby smear as he did so. "There I was, minding my own business, watching you and that little fella with you wandering off after you had met Granny and all of a sudden, I get this strange cold feeling like someone is walking on my grave... in big, frozen boots. I turns myself around and there's this big shadow on the wall and before I know it sucks me in and I wake up in this place..." he gestured around him at the teams of Humans, Sornette and Drömer digging and hammering despondently. "Since then I've been digging out chunks of rock like they told me."

"Who told you? Who is in charge here?" Lucid asked, reaching out his hand and resting it surprisingly gently on Carter's huge arm.

"The Supervisor, I suppose," Carter said, pointing to a squat figure more-or-less visible on the platform at the far end of the cavern. "He's the one that tells me where to work at least... he's the one that tells us all where to work... and he's the one that gathers up all the special stones." He paused and when he spoke again it was in hushed tones. "I don't think he's very nice..." As he finished speaking the figure in the distance turned towards them, and even at this distance Adam felt a chill run down his spine, the small figure emanating a surprising amount of malice.

"What special stones?" Lucid asked the large man, "what are they doing here?" But instead of answering Carter pulled his arm away, turned his back on them and made his way back across to the nearby boulders. He stopped in front of two gangly and under-fed looking Sornette, who were struggling to lift a large pick between the two of them, before gently taking it in a single hand and wandering over to the nearest pile of rock. Without any apparent effort he set about it, chips of stone flying out to either side and pinging off the nearest surface. Despite this very obvious and visible show of hard work, every now and then Adam could see Carter look nervously over his shoulder at the distant shape of the supervisor.

"Do you think..." Adam began, looking from Lucid to the pile of rusted tools piled haphazardly on the floor nearby.

"Yes... I suppose we should," Lucid sighed, picking up a particularly small Hammer and gesturing to Adam and Grimble to do the same, although every other available tool looked much larger and heavier. "Hiding in plain sight might be the best option. There are so many workers here that we should blend right in, just try your best to look hungry and miserable."

"Shouldn't be difficult," Adam sighed to himself.

Their progress was painfully slow. There were Nightmares all around the mining area, keeping a careful eye on the workers, despite their shackles. Every now and then there would be a momentary distraction, when one of the workers raised their arm with one of the odd stones clutched tightly, and Adam and his friends would scuttle from one working area to the next. The assorted Drőmer, Sornette, and others who were working in the mines seemed so despondent that they paid almost no attention to the new arrivals, keeping their heads down and concentrating on their work, refusing to say a word or even make eye contact.

This pattern continued for well over an hour, as Adam and his companions slowly made progress from one side of the cavern to the other. They had reached a point perhaps two-thirds of the way across when they were stopped short by another surprising reunion. The latest group of workers, clustered around a chunk of rock and hitting it with a complete lack of enthusiasm, were immediately familiar. Stood right in the centre was the unmistakable figure of Augustus Trimble, still in his Ringmaster's garb, although considerably dustier than the last time they had seen him. Around him were the rest of the odd troupe, the strongman punching the rock with his bare fists, the acrobat twins tapping away disdainfully with two hammers even smaller than the one Lucid had managed to find, and last but not least Oomba, the Drómer Cannonball, headbutting the rock with his crash helmet. As a group, they seemed to be making almost no impression on the rock at all, while managing at the same time to give off the impression of incredible hard work and effort.

Augustus was the first to see them, opening his mouth to shout a surprised greeting, but seeing Grimble's hasty shushing motion he clamped his jaw closed and raised a hand instead. Despite his silence, his shock at seeing them was clear, his eyes wide and full of questions. He tapped on the shoulders of each of his companions, pointing to Adam and the others while repeating Grimble's warning to stay quiet, which in the case of Oomba required him to hold his hand over his mouth for a good thirty seconds as he jumped up and down waving enthusiastically.

By the time Adam was stood directly next to him he risked a quiet whisper. "What in the Great Dream are you doing here... I mean how did you ever..."

Adam took a few minutes to explain what had happened since they had escaped, and then it was Augustus' turn to explain how he and the rest of the circus folk had ended up mining for the Nightmares. The story they shared was practically the same as Carter's. One by one the strange shadowy Nightmares had swallowed them up, despite their most valiant efforts, and they had found themselves here. Almost immediately they had been put to work and ever since they had spent all their time either mining or grabbing a few minutes to eat and sleep.

"I thought the food we had at the circus was bad," Oomba chimed in with a shudder, "but it was a delicious banquet compared to the horrible slop that passes for food in this place."

"What are they looking for?" Lucid asked, "It seems like a huge amount of effort for a few tiny stones."

"I don't know for sure," Augustus admitted. "None of us have managed to find a single one of the gems they are looking for."

"If you do find one you get double rations," Oomba added, "which is not as tempting a bonus as they seem to think."

Augustus shushed him. "But, although we haven't seen one first-hand, I have heard some of the others muttering about the stones being a source of energy for the Nightmares. Much as the Weave contains the memory of dreams, these stones contain the very essence of Nightmares, something that the Queen of this place is very keen to benefit from... or so the rumours suggest."

"Whatever it is she wants with them, I doubt it can be good," Grimble said, pulling absentmindedly on the longer hair around his chin.

"Regardless, we don't intend on staying here any longer than we have to," Lucid added. "Why don't you come with us?"

Augustus looked down with a sorrowful expression at the shackles around his legs and those of his companions. "I am afraid that it's a bit trickier for us to leave," he said, "and certainly not at any speed. It has been particularly trying for Pixie and Trixie."

Looking at the two acrobats, once so nimble and light on their feet, tethered to the ground and unable to do anything more than slowly shuffle around, Adam could understand how frustrated they must feel and why their faces told the most miserable story out of all of the circus troupe.

"Even if you can't come with us now, I promise that we will find a way to come back for you," Adam said, looking at Augustus but hoping that the others would also understand. "I haven't forgotten what you did for us on the ship... and there is no way that we are leaving you behind again."

"Pfft..." Augustus replied dismissively. "There was nothing more any of you could have done. All that would have happened is that you would be shackled now the same as us. Besides which, maybe you really will manage to find a way out of here, a way out for all of us." He looked across at the raised platform, jutting out over the caverns other exit. "But to leave you will have to pass right under the nose of the Overseer, and he is not a nice man."

He looked across at Oomba with a thoughtful look in his eyes. "Have you got any more tricks up your sleeve?" he asked.

The Drömer Cannonball patted down his pockets quickly. "They took pretty much everything I had," he replied, then with a grin he reached back into his mouth and pulled out a small waxed paper package. "But not quite everything... enough for maybe one more little explosion. Nothing fancy mind you."

"That should do. If you could package something up, and then I think..." Augustus looked back at the spot where the gigantic stone pillar continued its constant rhythm and nodded to himself. "Yes... that should do very nicely."

CHAPTER 14

As they ran helter-skelter down the steep stone corridor, the roar of pursuing Nightmares bouncing off the walls around them, Adam's mind replayed the chaos of the last few minutes. It had seemed like a good plan, or at least a better plan than they had before, (which was no plan at all), and to start off with it had looked like it was going to work.

Oomba had successfully packaged up the last of his gunpowder and passed it to Augustus, who had nonchalantly wandered slightly closer to the pillar, flicked the tiny flint that Grimble had given him and lit the small parcel, before throwing it across the ground. It had skimmed across the smooth rock of the cavern floor, bouncing once before coming to rest almost directly under the pillar. The stone column was currently at its highest point, dangling and ready to drop. The surrounding workers were all heaving on their heavy chains, waiting for the next drum-beat to sound.

Then the heavy thrumming sound of the drum reverberated around the cave and the chains were released once again, the stone column plummeting towards the ground as it had hundreds of times that morning. This time however its impact was much louder... and considerably more explosive than any of the previous times, hitting the ground just as the short fuse on Oomba's package fizzed through its last few centimetres.

It had turned out that Oomba's definition of 'nothing fancy' was a bit different to Adams. The explosion had been enormous, extremely loud and surprisingly colourful, with small sparks of various colours pinwheeling into the air mixed with shards of the stone pillar. Where presumably hundreds or even thousands of heavy impacts had failed to seriously damage the pillar, Oomba's package succeeded into completely demolishing the bottom third, bits of it now spinning dangerously across the cavern.

The initial explosive impact had been followed by an unhealthy and ominous creaking sound, as the scaffold which guided the stone column buckled slightly, leaving the pillar itself hanging slightly off to one side, swinging gently like a huge, unruly pendulum.

Admittedly, initially the distraction had worked as intended, every Nightmare in the place turning to watch the unfolding chaos, but unfortunately Adam had not been in the right place to take advantage of this. The explosion had been uncomfortably close, and it took a few seconds for the white spots to clear from in front of his eyes. After another thirty seconds or so the ringing in his ears had also faded enough for him to hear Lucid shouting, "RUN!"

Legs wobbling, he had followed Lucid and Grimble across the cave floor, past the last group of Nightmares and towards the welcome sight of the exit tunnel. Letting his gaze drift upwards for a moment, to the platform which sat over the exit, Adam could see the indistinct figure of the Overseer staring back down at him. While he couldn't make out much more than a short, shadowy outline, even at this distance its eyes stood out. They were large and round like an owl's, but coloured a deep red, and gave Adam the unshakable impression that while he couldn't see the Overseer very clearly the figure perched on the platform could see him, and everything else in the cavern extremely well.

"I think we've been rumbled," Adam had panted, still finding it hard to move at anything above a slow jog. "Whatever that thing up there is, I am pretty sure it has seen us and is probably not keen on us leaving." Almost immediately his concern had been proved correct, the sinister shape pointing down towards Adam and his friends and barking a muffled command of some kind.

Before anything further could happen, there had been a further pained creaking from the giant construct in the centre of the room. The supporting scaffold, already badly buckled and twisted, had chosen that exact moment to give up its uneven fight against the weight of the dangling pillar. With a final tortured screeching noise, the whole thing toppled slowly to one side, directly towards Adam, the Overseer and the wooden platform above the exit.

The next couple of minutes had been a complete blur. The scaffold had smashed straight through the wooden platform, which had been split almost completely in two, chunks of timber ricocheting across the chamber. Adam and his companions had just kept running, and more by luck than judgement had managed to make it through the carnage and into the welcome embrace of the exit tunnel without any major injury.

Although they had perhaps been lucky to get this far, their initial plan to use the explosion as a distraction had failed completely, and within moments pretty much every Nightmare in the place had started down to the passageway in pursuit. The barking shouts of the Overseer, who had survived the collapse of the wooden platform and risen from the wreckage like a squat, vengeful bird of prey, bounced off the walls around them.

Bringing his attention back to the present, Adam realised to his dismay that they had run down a dead end, and it was only by skidding uncomfortably to a halt next to Lucid and nearly losing his footing that he managed to avoid running headfirst into a blank but very solid looking stone wall. A moment later Grimble also drew to a halt next to him, leaning against the wall, alternating between gasping to regain his breath and muttering a variety of colourful Drőmer curses.

The sounds of the pursuing Nightmares were growing louder in the passageway behind them, a mix of roars, hisses and unpleasant slithering noises that made Adam's skin crawl. Crouching down, with one hand pressed against the blank rockface to steady himself, Adam tried to decide on a Daydream he could use. To his side Grimble was rapidly patting down his various pockets and pouches, hoping that he could find some potion or powder that had survived their abrupt landing and subsequent adventures. From his increasingly loud grumbling, it didn't sound like there was much he could use.

Fighting down growing feelings of panic, Adam concentrated as hard as he was able, and looking down at his arm could see the Daydream taking effect, the skin of his hand turning slowly into interlocking plates of metal. Within a few seconds, the sensation of solidity had spread over his whole body and he rose, slightly unsteadily and with an unusual clanking sound.

"What in the Great Dream?" Grimble gasped, looking at Adam's altered form and pausing his frantic search for one, open-mouthed moment.

"Haven't you ever seen a robot before?" Adam asked, his voice coming out as an emotionless monotone that he struggled to recognise as his own.

"Obviously not," Grimble grunted, "whatever one of them is."

"Maybe an explanation for another time," Adam replied, bracing his feet as firmly as he could and raising two large metal hands in what he hoped was an intimidating fighting pose.

The noises from down the passageway had intensified considerably, now so loud and frantic it almost sounded like the Nightmares were fighting amongst themselves. Several of the hisses and other noises that had made up the unpleasant cacophony of sound had stopped, and moments later there was a final loud roar before a sudden and ominous silence took its place.

There was a heavy footstep from just around the corner, almost directly in front of the small alcove where Adam, Lucid and Grimble had inadvertently trapped themselves, so heavy in fact that the ground tremored ever so slightly.

"That's not good," Grimble muttered, raising his hands to show the best he had been able to salvage from his pockets, which in this case looked like a handful of rather limp dried plants, unlikely to achieve anything other than giving the approaching Nightmare a slight allergic reaction. Lucid had even less to offer, although he was still holding the tiny hammer that he had picked up in the mine.

There was another thunderous step and a huge and extremely dangerous looking clawed hand appeared, grasping the corner of the wall directly in front of them. Seeing the sharp talons scratching deep grooves in the solid stone of the wall, Adam wished he had Daydreamed something bigger than his current choice. Something much, much larger... like a battleship.

Gulping he clenched his metal fists, which didn't look quite as impressive as they had a moment ago, and then the Nightmare drew fully into view.

Although the passageway was pretty large, a good three metres from floor to ceiling and nearly as wide, the Nightmare creature had to crouch to fit, shoulders hunched and neck bowed. It was without a doubt the biggest and most unpleasant Nightmare that Adam had seen so far in Reverie, reminding him of several of his worst dreams rolled into one giant, horrible package. The face in particular drew Adam's attention, with four huge, glowing eyes and a mouth so full of massive fangs that they didn't all fit, several of the large teeth protruding from the gaping maw at awkward angles. As it turned its full attention to them the mouth twisted into a satisfied smile. Bubbling saliva dribbled from the corner of its lips, which hissed and fizzled as it made contact with the stone floor, leaving it discoloured and slightly melted.

There was a gentle whooshing sound off to Adam's side and Grimble's handful of plants span slowly through the air before hitting the creature and then drifting down to the ground. This was followed by a gentle 'plink' as Lucid's miniature hammer bounced off the Nightmares tough skin. Risking a quick look to his right Adam saw Lucid and Grimble both give slightly embarrassed shrugs, before turning his attention back to the beast now only metres from them.

All four of the oddly shaped eyes were looking intently at him. Steeling himself Adam tried to meet the gaze and look as intimidating as he could manage. He wasn't sure if robots were supposed to sweat, but he was pretty sure he was managing it all the same. Either that or he was leaking some kind of oil.

The massive jaws opened wide, showing the full range of jagged, spiky, shiny and generally horrible teeth. At the same time, the creature extended one huge arm, ridged with sinewy muscle, long clawed fingers extended.

"Pleased to meet you," the creature muttered, "and... um... sorry about the mess."

"Sorry... about the mess...?" Adam parroted back, completely confused.

"Yes, all the fighting and chasing and everything," the monster replied, somehow managing to look embarrassed despite its otherwise horrifying appearance. "I was hoping that we would meet under nicer circumstances."

The giant clawed hand was still extended and to Adam's great surprise he found himself reaching out to meet it. As he did so he let his Daydream go and the metal plates that covered him faded, replaced once again with soft skin. When the creature gripped his palm it was incredibly gentle. Its touch was both warmer and less unpleasant than Adam had feared.

He was pretty sure that the Nightmare gave a shy smile as they gingerly shook hands. "I'm Sktthytthx," the creature hissed, managing a noise that Adam was pretty sure human vocal chords would never be able to do justice to, "but you can call me Simon."

CHAPTER 15

"Simon?" Adam repeated, still thinking that he must have hit his head during their escape and expecting to wake up at any moment.

"It's my 'friendly' name," Simon said. "Mittens said we should all pick a 'friendly' name and I chose Simon..." His four eyes narrowed in concern. "That's okay, isn't it... I mean it's a good name?"

For a giant monster, he looked remarkably like a worried puppy and Adam's first reaction had been to reassure him that his name was exceedingly friendly, but as soon as he heard the name 'Mittens' all other thoughts were shoved to the back of his head.

"Did you just say Mittens?" he asked incredulously, his mind sprinting back to the time he had spent with the Incubo that Nora had brought back with her from the Dreamworld. Although he had initially been highly suspicious of her, and her claims that she was one of a group of Nightmares that opposed some of the worst things happening in Reverie, she had proved herself to be a reliable ally time and time again. She had still been scary, and not exactly 'good' in the traditional sense of the word, but she had saved them all on more than one occasion, and by the end of their time together Adam had been surprised at how sad he'd felt seeing her leave.

"Yeah," Simon told him, nodding his scaly head. "She's the one that said to look out for you. We've been searching for you and your friends." He paused and looked around at the group. "I suppose that makes me the lucky one. Come with me, Mittens and the others will want to see you."

"Others?"

"Oh yes," Simon said, "you and your friends are the reasons that the Triple F came to exist in the first place." As he said this he crossed two of the huge, taloned fingers and raised his left hand. Seeing Adam staring at his hand, he added. "That's the secret sign we use... um... I'm not sure I was supposed to show you that." His massive brow furrowed. "When you meet Mittens could you pretend you don't know about the sign?"

"Sure... I suppose," Adam replied, feeling like he had entered a weird parallel dimension, or at least an even weirder parallel dimension than normal.

"Follow me," Simon told him as he began to lumber up the corridor. It was hard to keep up, Simon's massive limbs making his natural walking speed much faster than Adam or even Lucid could manage without running. Grimble was having an even worse time, having to sprint to keep anywhere close to the rest, wheezing uncontrollably after the first few minutes. Despite his shortness of breath, he still managed to maintain an almost constant stream of grumbles and insults aimed at Simon's huge, scaly back.

The only time he would stop was when Simon looked over his shoulder to make sure that they were still following, giving them all an encouraging, toothy smile. During those moments Grimble would grin back, giving him an insincere thumbs up, which would vanish as soon as Simon looked away.

After nearly half an hour of alternately jogging and sprinting down a variety of very similar looking stone passages, which had left Adam completely lost and Grimble wheezing like a broken and waterlogged set of bagpipes, Simon suddenly drew to a halt.

"We're here," he told them, smiling at them through his astounding set of fangs. "Now try not to be nervous, there are some fairly scary looking characters here, but they are all really nice once you get to know them."

He was answered with a variety of semi-positive sounding gasps and wheezes from Adam and his companions, who were all in various stages of exhaustion. Adam did manage a half-hearted smile back, although at the back of his mind he was getting quite worried that Simon, who was about the most awful Nightmare he had ever seen, had described the group that they were about to meet as "fairly scary."

While he didn't want to appear rude, Adam was pretty sure that anything Simon felt to be "fairly scary," was probably going to be the most terrible sight in the world, so he steeled himself for the worst and took a deep breath as Simon pressed his claws against an innocent looking outcrop of rock. There was a momentary pause, after which a section of the previously solid looking wall shuddered and then slowly swung inwards, leaving a doorway sized opening.

The room they entered wasn't exactly what he had been expecting. In fact, it was so far from the image he had in his mind, which was filled with visions of dark shadows, tall dribbly candles and dark, sinister-looking furniture, that Adam was stopped dead in his tracks.

Rather than a shadowy cavern, the room looked more like a granny's living room. Right in the centre was a large table, topped with a lace-edged tablecloth that didn't quite fit the table-top, leaving the far edges uncovered. Even more disturbingly, someone's rather optimistic interpretation of a tea-set, but one which had been blown up to a scale more suited to Simon's massive hands, took centre-stage of the odd display. There was a watering-can, painted white and detailed with some flowers daubed enthusiastically across it, which Adam took to be the teapot, around which were a range of large bowls, pans, and other random items, which seemed to be serving the function of teacups.

There was a polite sounding cough from off to one side, and he managed to tear his eyes away from the table-top to look at the rest of the room. All around the table were a series of comfy looking armchairs of various shapes, sizes, and floral patterns, and each one contained a hulking Nightmare figure. To his immediate right was a tall, rather gangly Nightmare who gave Adam what he assumed was meant to be a friendly grin, raising a massive tea-cup (this one looking disturbingly like a re-purposed chamber pot), in greeting. Its teeth were even more impressive than Simon's and appeared to be dripping with some sort of corrosive bile. Adam had to fight the impulse to gag slightly as he gave a tentative smile back.

"Welcome," it grunted at him, a greeting which was echoed around the room in a range of gurgles, warbles, and rasps.

"Um, hi," Adam managed, waving rather haphazardly around the room.

At the far end of the table there was a scraping sound as a particularly brightly patterned armchair was pushed back and a familiar figure rose to her feet.

"Mittens," Adam said, his discomfort forgotten at the sight of his old companion. She had taken the form of a slick, oily version of Nora, as she had the very last time they had spoken, just before she'd left Adam and his friends. He had no idea whether she had chosen that form to make them feel more comfortable, or just because she had grown to like it, but for the moment he decided not to ask.

Seeing her now, surrounded by a rag-tag group of Nightmares, all looking like they were desperately trying to act in what they assumed to be a civilised manner, Adam presumed this was where her quest had taken her. It wasn't exactly what he had expected, but he was strangely fascinated by the odd scene and was increasingly curious to hear exactly what he and his friends had walked into.

"I'm so glad that Simon managed to find you," Mittens told him. "Please take a seat and perhaps I will be able to explain what's going on."

Adam, Lucid and Grimble all managed to squeeze into a single seat, which was surprisingly comfortable, although they did also

129

politely but very firmly turn down the offer of a drink from the massive tea-pot.

"So," Lucid began, leaning forward and resting his chin on long-fingered hands, "what's all this about?"

"This," Mittens told them, spreading her hands out wide, taking in the room and the surrounding audience of Nightmares, who were now sat in silence, "this is the headquarters of the Freedom from Fear organisation, or the Triple F as some know it". As she said this, from the corner of his eye Adam saw several of the seated Nightmares making the same crossed fingers symbol that Simon had made earlier.

"As I told you before we parted company," she continued, "the more I stayed in Reverie the more it became obvious that there was further work for me to do here. Too many times Nightmares, Incubo like my friends here, have been made to do things outside of the rules of this world."

The silence around the room gave way to muttered agreements and grunts of support.

"So, I found others who felt the same way and we formed this group."

"And what does 'your group' do exactly?" Grimble asked, his gruff voice cutting over the background rumblings.

"We watch and learn what we can," Mittens told them. "We find out what the Queen and her cohorts are planning and then we try and stick a spanner in the works."

"The Queen?"

"Yes, Ephialtes. Queen of all the Nightmares. She is the centre of power on this side of Reverie, her and her favourites. You know them well enough. Isenbard and Chimera."

Adam's blood ran cold at the mention of two names that he recognised all too well. He had known, deep down, hidden away in a part of his brain that he ignored as much as he could, that both

Isenbard and Chimera were likely to return at some point. Neither had been seen since their defeat, Isenbard disappearing along with the swirling Horror he had brought into the world and Chimera vanishing into the collapsing ruins of the palace in Moonshine, but it had been too much to hope that they were gone for good.

"The Queen rules this place completely, her power is absolute, but until recently she operated within the rules of the Great Dream," Mittens continued. "But something changed and now she constantly pushes in every direction to extend her power, always with an eye on the rest of Reverie and in particular the Stairway of Dreams." She scowled as unpleasant thoughts worked their way into the forefront of her mind. "My fellow Incubo are made to do things that go beyond reason. Her henchmen are almost as bad, using Nightmares as their own personal armies. They hate the Stairway nearly as much as she does."

One of the others seated around the table piped up, although piped was probably the wrong way to describe the deep, rasping rumble. "She is clever, she knows what it is that people want, what makes them tick deep inside. It's why Isenbard and Chimera are so loyal to her, whatever in the world they want the most... you can be sure that's what she is offering them."

Adam thought back to the times he had encountered them both, each one driven by something slightly out of their control. Isenbard had been desperate to break through into the Waking World, while Chimera had been driven by his need to purge what he had seen as an impurity in his blood. He guessed that each one was so hungry, so desperate that they would do pretty much anything the Queen asked of them if it got them closer to their goal. For the briefest of moments, he felt a pang of sympathy for them, both chasing something that he suspected they would never be able to reach. Then he reminded himself just how far they had been willing to go, how many people they had been willing to hurt, and the sympathy vanished, compressed and crystalised into something harder.

"So, that's what we are," Mittens concluded. "A speck of grit in the Queen's eye, a pebble in her shoe. We might not be strong enough to topple her, or even be that much of a threat, but we slow her down at every opportunity... and perhaps one day..." she stopped without finishing her sentence, changing the subject.

"Which brings us to you, what are you and your friends doing so far from home. I heard that a human had been spotted and there was only one human that I knew that would be so foolish. So we have been looking for you, hoping to find you before the Queen's allies."

Adam shot a quick sideways look to Grimble and Lucid. He trusted Mittens completely, they had been through too much together not to. But it still felt strange to share the details of their quest with a room full of Incubo, traditionally their sworn enemies.

Lucid nodded at him. "We need their help. We are far from home and I doubt we would have got even this far without Simon's timely intervention."

Across the room, Simon blushed deeply, or at least the scales on his face went a bit redder, muttering something about, "it being nothing really."

"It's what you told me last time we spoke, just before you left," Adam said. "You told me that my Mum was somewhere here. It took a while to find a way to cross the ocean and get here, but we managed it." He paused, aware that the full attention of the room was on him.

"But on the way here we ran into a new kind of Nightmare, patches of shadow that swallow people up, worse than any I have seen before." His mind went back to the brief battle on the Pirate ship and he shuddered at the memory of the way the strange circus crew had been swallowed up, one after another

"We have seen them too," Mittens told him. "Creations of the Queen's own dark imagination. Any poor soul sucked into the darkness is brought here. If they are lucky then they are put to work in the mines."

"And if they are not?" Grimble asked.

Mittens didn't reply, instead, she looked down at the ground for a moment before making eye contact with Adam again.

"We don't know for sure, we tried to find out and... it did not end well."

She didn't seem willing to explain any further, and Adam didn't want to press her on something that seemed to cause her painful memories.

"So, we have told you why we are here," Grimble said, breaking the rather bleak silence, "are you able to help?"

"More than you might imagine," Mittens told him, clicking her fingers. "Very recently we crossed paths with someone that you know only too well."

One of the Incubo at the far end of the room gave her a nod and made their way out through a small doorway that Adam hadn't previously paid much attention to.

After a couple of minutes, spent in near complete silence, with Adam, Lucid and Grimble exchanging the occasional awkward glance, the door swung open again. But this time rather than the looming figure of the Incubo that had left the room, the silhouetted figure was much smaller and almost immediately familiar.

"Mum?" Adam said in disbelief, although it came out as nothing more than a strangled grunt. His throat felt like it had closed-up, making it hard to breathe, let alone speak.

But it was her, despite his doubts. It seemed impossible after so long spent searching, that she should just walk into the room like it was nothing, but every single detail was as fresh and familiar to Adam as his own face in the mirror each morning. There was the same wide, slightly wonky smile, the same laughter lines gently etched around her eyes. But despite all the comfortable areas of familiarity, Adam could also see that their time apart had taken its toll on his mother. Her hair was tightly tied back and her face looked thinner, more tired than he remembered. There was also an underlying hardness to her that he didn't recognise, something steely behind the welcoming smile.

Through a mist Adam approached her with his arms outstretched, reaching out for the comfort of a hug he had crossed worlds to find.

When he finally found himself enclosed once again in her arms, she hugged him so hard that it made his ribs hurt, but he didn't complain. The moment seemed to stretch on forever, everything else fading far into the background, shifting out of focus. All that mattered was that their tiny, perfect family was reunited. Adam could feel an uncomfortable dampness on his neck and realised that his mum was crying. Pulling away from her in alarm he looked up to see what was wrong and realised that she was smiling through the tears.

"Look at you," she said. "You look so different, so grown up... I haven't been gone that long... have I?" She paused for a moment, looking genuinely concerned.

"No, it's not been that long, a few months maybe," Adam replied. "A few, very busy, very weird months." Looking into his mother's eyes, stained red with emotion, he asked the question that had been burning within him since she had first disappeared, a tiny flickering candle of doubt that he hadn't been able to extinguish.

"Why didn't you come back? I know you came here to escape from Isenbard... but we defeated him months ago... and you never came back."

Despite his happiness at finally seeing his mum again, it was hard to make his words sound like anything other than an accusation.

"I know," his mum replied gently, reaching out again and grasping Adam by his shoulders, giving them a reassuring squeeze. "I understand... I wanted to come back... I wanted to be back with you, but I couldn't." Letting go of Adam, she let her arms drop to her sides and then lowered herself into one of the empty seats, looking suddenly tired. As she sat Adam saw the occasional strand of grey mixed in with the more familiar blond of her hair and wondered how steep a price she had paid, spending so long away from her life in the 'real' world.

"Why not?" Adam asked her. "Why couldn't you come back?"

"The pendant you wear around your neck, the one you keep with you all the time. It's what gives you your link to Reverie."

Adam nodded, remembering when he had first found the pendant in his mum's room just before waking for the very first time in the Great Dream. His hand slipped unconsciously to the spot where it nestled safely under his t-shirt. He felt it give off a pulse of warmth, reminding him that there were other questions that he had for his mother.

"Well, I had something too, something that was important to me... and that was my link between the worlds. I had a ring. It was small and cheap, really quite tacky, with a coloured glass gemstone." His mum smiled at the recollection. "I won it in one of those grabbing-arm games at the funfair when I was about your age. I used nearly a month's pocket money for something only worth a few pence, but I loved it. I wore it all the time, including the very first time I came to Reverie. It didn't take too long to work out that if I wasn't wearing it when I fell asleep my night would be boring and uneventful, but when I did, I came here and..."

She drew to a close before finishing her sentence. She didn't need to explain the wonders of the Dream World to Adam.

"Soon enough, as I grew older, I outgrew it and had to wear it on my little finger. I never took it off, never let it leave my sight. But when I fled here the last time... I lost it, or more precisely it was stolen from me. When I escaped from Isenbard, rather than appearing near Nocturne, as I always had before, I ended up here and... she was waiting for me."

She shuddered slightly as she continued. "Ephialtes, the Queen of Nightmares... somehow she knew where I would be and tried to trap me here. I managed to escape... just. But I lost my ring during my escape and I am pretty sure that she has it now. Without it, I can't get back to our world, but I'm not strong enough to take it back from her, so ever since I have been stuck here, running and hiding. I have helped you when I could, even without my ring I can manage a decent Daydream or two, but it's getting harder and harder to hold on."

She stopped her explanation and slowly rolled up her shirt sleeve and Adam heard Lucid draw a sharp inward breath beside him. For a moment he couldn't see what had caused Lucid's reaction, then he spotted it too. Halfway up his mother's arm there was a patch, a little bigger than the base of a teacup, where the skin of her arm was completely transparent. There was no visible flesh or bone under the missing patch, just a blank emptiness as if there was nothing under her skin at all.

His mum gave a wry smile. "I have been here too long, unable to return back to our world. For a while it was fine, I was safe here... so long as they couldn't find me in the Waking World... and I had found a hiding place, somewhere I could sleep safely for a good long time."

She looked down at her arm, at the patch where her skin had started to become transparent and shook her head sadly.

"But a while ago this started. Unless I can find my way back soon then I will fade away bit by bit. I have already been asleep far, far longer than anyone should ever be able to manage. My Daydreaming has kept me safe, kept me alive, but even with that... in the end..."

She rolled her sleeve back down, covering the transparent patch and managed to scrape a smile back onto her face. "Don't look so sad... it's fine," she said. "I didn't think I would see you again and now I have. Somehow you made it all the way here, further than anyone in Reverie has ever travelled. I am so very, very proud."

Her words were buzzing in Adam's ears, making him feel sick and giddy. It was impossible, completely unfair. To have travelled so far and done so much only to find out that his mum was going to fade away right in front of his eyes. Even worse than that was the way his mum spoke about it, like she was already resigned to the fate she had described and was just trying to find a gentle way of saying goodbye.

"So, what do you need, how do you get back?" Adam asked, determined not to let any emotion slip through the cracks in his voice.

"My ring is the only way," his mum said quietly, "and Ephialtes has it."

"Then we'll get it back."

"No!" the suddenness and strength of his mum's voice made Adam jump. "Absolutely not. She is far too dangerous for you to go anywhere near."

"But..." Adam began, unable to shake the image of the transparent spot on his mum's arm from his mind.

"But nothing," his mum replied, more calmly but still extremely firmly. "I shouldn't have even mentioned it. The only important thing is that you are here... and that we are together."

The rest of the evening passed with his mum insisting that Adam told her everything that had happened to him since he had first entered Reverie. Although he suspected that she already knew many of the details, she listened keenly to every word, leaning forward and staring at him across the giant table, her chin resting on her hands. Her eyes shone with pride throughout and she gasped with surprise or grinned with excitement at all the right moments, to the degree that, for a short while, they were both caught away in the rushing tides of his adventures and Adam almost forgot about his worries.

It was an odd feeling, to be the one telling, rather than listening to stories, bringing back warm memories of the tales his mum had shared with him every night before bed. It took him back to a time when his dreams had been limited to happy picture shows in his sleeping mind, rather than the doorway to the extraordinary double life he now led.

After several hours of talking, and one large cup of a strange drink that looked a bit like tea but tasted like a burning mattress, Adam's mum pushed herself back from the table with a regretful sounding sigh. "Sorry Adam," she said, "but I think I am going to have to go to bed. I get tired a lot quicker than I used to. We can carry on tomorrow. For now, you should probably try and sleep too, have some time back in the Waking World, catch up with Charlie or maybe go and see Nora." She smiled hopefully at the end of the last comment and Adam hadn't the heart to tell her that Nora pretty much hated him.

There were so many questions that Adam still had for her, that he hadn't managed to find the words to ask yet. About the pendant, about his past and his father, but he knew they would have to wait for another day, for a time when he and his mother were alone and could dig down into the things that really mattered.

After a final, long and heartfelt hug his mum wished him good night and made her way back out of the meeting room, although to Adam's unspoken worry she had to lean heavily on the broad, scaly arm of one of the Nightmares as she did so.

One after another the Nightmares who had remained in the room also said their various goodbyes until only Adam, Lucid, Grimble and Mittens were left.

"Well, finding your mum was easier than I thought it might be," Grimble began, patting Adam on the arm awkwardly.

"She's dying, isn't she…" Adam said flatly, shrugging off Grimble's well-meaning gesture and instead locking eyes with Mittens across the table.

"She is… unwell," Mittens admitted, having the good grace to look down for a moment as she answered. "She has been in this world far too long, and despite her incredible strength it has finally started to catch up with her. But seeing you today put a smile on her face that I haven't seen before."

"I don't care about making her smile," Adam replied, then shook his head. "That's not what I mean… what I meant is I didn't come all this way… I didn't find her, just to watch her fade away into nothingness. I came here so we could go home together… and that is what we are going to do."

Mittens raised an enquiring eyebrow, with the sharp edge of a smile on her lips. "So what do you propose… Daydreamer?"

"You point me in the direction of this Queen," Adam said firmly. "Show me where to go and I will find her, I will get my mum's ring back and then I will take her home like I promised."

Mittens' smile broadened, revealing a row of sharp, pointy teeth quite unlike Nora's. "Bravo," she said, clapping her hands together enthusiastically. "Nice to see that you're still as brave as I remember."

"The word you're looking for is stupid," Grimble muttered from behind Adam. "Brave is just another word for someone who manages to combine stupid with lucky." He sighed, and his next words were surprisingly sincere. "But on this occasion, even I would have to agree with you. We can't just watch your mother fade away, so what do you suggest?"

"I'm going to leave tonight, as soon as possible," Adam said, trying to clear his mind of its own tumultuous thoughts as he spoke. He did his best to push the momentary happiness he had felt, sat swapping stories with his mum, from his mind, painfully aware that having only just found her he was planning on leaving her once again. "I don't expect you to come with me, you have both done enough already, and this Ephialtes sounds dangerous."

"I'm afraid you can't stop me from joining you," Lucid cracked the knuckles of his long fingers as he stood up. "In case you have forgotten I have known your mother since she was a child, I wouldn't allow harm to come to her any more than you would." Although his voice remained calm and friendly, Adam could see the determination in his friend's expression, a hardness that settled over the normally soft features of his face.

"If you don't mind, I think I will stay here," Grimble added after a few moments of thought. "Don't misunderstand me, I'm with you all the way on this... Dreamer help me, but I think I might be of most use here. Perhaps I can find a way to help your mother, some potion or treatment that will help slow whatever it is that is making her fade. Apparently Mittens and her friends have quite a well-stocked store, I may find something I can use"

Adam reached and clutched the arm of his short Drómer companion with gratitude. "Thank-you," he said. "I know you will do whatever you can to keep her safe and well until I get back."

"Okay, enough of the heroic speeches from you lot," Mittens broke in, pulling a pained face and miming retching. "I might be reformed, but all this self-sacrifice and camaraderie is making me feel a bit sick. If you are going to look for Ephialtes then I suggest you get moving." She walked over to the small doorway that his mum had used to enter the room earlier.

"Follow me."

With a final nod to Grimble, Adam and Lucid followed her out of the room and into the passageway beyond. For the next ten minutes, they followed Mittens closely as she took one turning after another until they had lost all sense of direction. Then as suddenly as she had started, she drew to a halt by a fork in the current passage.

"This is where we part ways," she informed them, pointing down the left-hand split in the passage. "I need to get back... and you need to go down there."

"Are you not coming with us?" Adam asked, surprised at how bothered he was about Mittens leaving.

"Sorry Adam," she replied, and there seemed to be genuine regret in the glistening black pools of her eyes. "I would, but there are a lot of Nightmares that are relying on me, and I have to look after them. They might be big and tough and scary, but they don't really know what they are doing. This rebellion doesn't come naturally to them, and without me..."

Adam thought back to the hunched Nightmares clustered around the strange dinner table, gnarled and scaled, gruesome and monstrous and yet painfully keen to make Adam and his friends feel welcome.

"I understand," he said. "Thanks for bringing us this far... and for looking after my mum."

"Of course," Mittens replied, then with a quick wave started heading back in the direction they had come from. "Good luck to you."

"Wait," Lucid shouted at her retreating back. "How will we find our way back?"

Mittens smiled her familiar toothy grin. "Just click your heels together and say, "there's no place like home"."

"What... really?" Adam began to ask, then stopped himself as his brain caught up with his mouth.

He stood and watched as Mittens disappeared around the nearest corner, her trailing shadow changing from the familiar outline of Nora to something bigger and much, much more terrible, then he turned back to Lucid. "Right then," he said. "We have an evil Nightmare Queen to face, so we may as well get going."

For the first few minutes of their journey little changed from the mixture of passageways and caves that they had experienced so far, each one very similar to the last, although there were no further splits in the route to choose between, just one long and continuous sequence of dark stone walls and enclosed, claustrophobic caverns.

Just as Adam was starting to think that they were stuck in some never-ending loop of identical passages, they stumbled across something new. This cavern was far bigger than any of those that Adam and Lucid had previously passed through. Also different was the light, rather than the grimy darkness of the other caves, this one was lit by the first rays of the morning light spilling down through an opening high above them.

The reason for that opening became clear as soon as they started to make their way through the cave, or as it turned out, stables. Tethered to large steel rods, driven deep into the rock, were fierce looking creatures that reminded Adam of large horses. Although only if horses were surrounded by a cloud of dark, billowing smoke that clung close to their skin and had long, bat-like wings folded up tight on either side of their body... and eyes that glowed with a deep red malice.

"Mara," Lucid murmured with a scowl. "It would have been nice if Mittens had thought it worth mentioning. Whatever you do move slowly and don't draw more attention to yourself than you need to."

"What?"

"They are Mara," Lucid replied in hushed tones, flapping his hands for Adam to also keep his voice down. "They are the steeds of Nightmares, very loyal, very intelligent and very, very bad-tempered. So, like I just said, keep things slow and quiet and we might not get trampled to death."

After a very quick look across at Lucid to make sure he wasn't joking, the sudden sweat on his brow making it pretty clear that he was serious, Adam slowed his pace to match that of his friend, who was now moving with exaggerated caution between the stalls housing the creatures. Occasionally one would pull at its tether, or give a low groaning sound as they passed, but it seemed that as long as they didn't trouble the Mara, the Nightmare steeds wouldn't trouble them.

Despite this, both Adam and Lucid didn't dare to even breathe heavily until they were all the way across the stables and safe in the next tunnel. Leaning against the wall and letting his nerves settle, Adam looked across at his friend, who was wiping his brow with a small handkerchief.

"This place doesn't seem to end," Adam said, rather despondently. "It just keeps going on and on. First the mines, then this place... and none of it is nice."

"It seems we have stumbled, either by accident or some design of the Dreamer himself, into the very heartland of the Nightmares," Lucid replied. "The Mara are the favoured steed of the Queen herself, reserved for her use and that of her most favoured subjects. So, wherever we have found ourselves, it is likely we are close to her." He paused, putting his sweat-stained handkerchief back in his pocket. "I don't honestly know if that's a good or bad thing."

"Well we're not going to get my mum's ring back without finding her," Adam replied, with far more bravado than he genuinely felt. He gestured down the passageway, to where it looked like it opened out into yet another cavern. "Perhaps this is it, maybe we have found where the Queen is."

As Adam and Lucid crept their way to the end of the passage and took a peek into the next expansive cave, Adam's breath caught in his throat. It looked like his prediction had been more accurate than he had first realised.

There, right in the centre of the cavern was a throne, tall and slender, rising straight out of the stone, formed of the same dark rock, glistening where the flickering lights caught the seams of crystal running in slim bands through it.

The figure sat on the throne was as thin as the surrounding shards of rock, long arms resting on the padded velvet rests that adorned the hard stone. Each limb ended in skeletal fingers with long, sharp nails tapping a constant impatient tempo. Although he couldn't make out every detail from so far away, Adam could see that the seated figure was a woman, almost impossibly slender. Long robes of red and black swathed her, running down the throne, extending for several metres in every direction. Her hair was long, dark and lustrous, almost glowing with life and vitality in direct contrast to the rest of her, with her face gaunt and worn, cheekbones hollow and eyes deeply set.

Although Adam was pretty sure that there was no way she could possibly see him from so far away, her head swivelled towards the spot where he and Lucid were sheltered, face tilted back slightly, as if she was sniffing the air.

"Welcome Daydreamer." When the Queen spoke, her voice far sweeter and melodious than her emaciated appearance would have suggested. It carried across the vast cavern with far more strength than should have been possible, sounding as clear as if she was standing next to them, rather than hundreds of metres away. "Don't just stand there hiding in the shadows like a scared little mouse. Come out from your hidey-hole and we can talk."

She raised one skinny arm and turning her hand over, beckoned with one long, curling fingernail.

Although he really, really, didn't want to, there didn't seem to be much point in carrying on hiding, so reluctantly Adam peeled himself away from the comforting darkness of the tunnel.

As he stepped into the light of the vast cavern Adam could feel the gaze of a hundred Nightmares burning his skin. Although he was determined that he wouldn't show any nerves, it seemed this message hadn't got through to his legs, which were objecting strenuously to every step he took towards the throne.

"I am a Daydreamer," Adam muttered to himself, "so they are every bit as scared of me as I am of them." Despite this internal pep-talk, it seemed that the massed Nightmares were extremely good at hiding their fear. Instead of looking frightened of Adam and Lucid as they walked past, they looked fierce, angry or in some particularly horrifying cases, just plain hungry.

One of the scariest looking Incubo, with the head of a badger on the body of a gorilla, (which was a far more terrifying combination than it might sound), gave Adam a discreet wink and made the surreptitious sign for the Triple F with its left hand.

Making a particularly hard effort not to react, Adam managed to keep his expression neutral, but amongst all the surrounding horribleness, the friendly sign did make him feel slightly better, despite it being given by a hand which looked capable of unscrewing his head like a bottle top.

As they reached the base of the rocky outcrop which formed the throne, Adam was able to get a closer look at the woman sat there. The first impressions of incredible thinness were visibly reinforced now he was right by her. The face looking down at him with an expression of amused curiosity was almost skeletal, with dark, emotionless eyes set in sunken sockets above a long, slim nose.

"That's better," she purred, thin lips lifting in a satisfied smile, "now we can talk properly, like civilised people."

Gathering up his courage and trying to ignore the spiky stares of dozens of angry Nightmares prickling his back, Adam did his best to answer, although when he did his voice was weaker and more highly pitched than he intended.

"I didn't come here to talk. I came to get my mum's ring back. The ring you stole."

"Ha... brave words young man," the Queen replied, seeming genuinely impressed, "well done indeed."

She raised one of her bony arms and wiggled her fingers impatiently at one of the closest Nightmares who gave an awkward low bow, before scuttling off, disappearing amongst the throng of other gathered monsters.

"I do have your mother's ring, you are quite correct, although I must say, I am a little disappointed that she hasn't come to claim it herself." She tapped long, dark fingernails against one of the stone armrests, humming to herself, before turning back to Adam and smiling another, rather unpleasant smile. "Although perhaps she might show herself for the sake of her son if he found himself in some sort of terrible danger..." This last comment was met with a deep, appreciative roar from the surrounding horde of Nightmares.

Adam gulped, preparing for some sort of attack, and he could tell that Lucid was also tensing himself, but it seemed that Ephialtes hadn't finished.

"But... no, that would be discourteous of me, especially after you have come all this way," she mused, half to herself. "I am sure you have terrible notions of what I might be, some sort of cruel monster, but I am far from that. I have something that you want, and you have the ability to help me regain something that is of equal importance to me. There is absolutely no need for us to fight, instead, I believe that we can achieve much more with a simple trade."

"What could you possibly need that we could help you with?" Lucid broke in, his voice thick with obvious distaste.

"Hush," Ephialtes replied, "I was talking to my new little friend here, not to you." As she spoke, she reached up with one bony hand and pulled a strand of her long, dark hair taut, before slicing it cleanly through with a talon-like fingernail. As it slowly snaked its way towards the ground she blew gently, and it drifted across the room.

By the time it covered the short distance between the Queen and where Adam and Lucid were standing it had grown to several metres in length, and before either one of them could react it had wrapped itself several times around Lucid's body. The rapidly constricting band drew his arms tightly into his body, after which it wormed its way up his neck, before completely and effectively gagging him.

"That's better," Ephialtes sighed, turning her attention back to Adam. "Now, while we wait for my servants to return with the ring you are so keen to find, there's a story I wanted to share with you."

"Let my friend go!" Adam cried, clenching his fists by his side, his previous nerves burned away by the hot anger he could feel bubbling through his veins.

"No... I most certainly will not," Ephialtes replied quite calmly, making a small, bored gesture with one hand. Off to Adam's side, he heard Lucid give a sharp intake of pained breath as the dark bands encircling him tightened. "And if you interrupt me again without permission it will go very badly for your tall, rude friend."

Teeth clenched, biting back the words he wanted to say, Adam nodded silently instead and slowly let his fury subside. Out the corner of his eye he was relieved to see Lucid relax slightly as the pressure on him was reduced, although what Adam could see of his face was still filled with scarcely contained panic.

"Good... glad to see that you have some sense. Now we can begin the story without any further interference." Ephialtes began in a sing-song voice, "Once upon a time, in a land far, far away there lived a young boy and his even younger sister. They lived an enviable life with their family. A happy childhood spent playing games and having extraordinary adventures. One day they would be pirates, the next great explorers, every day something new and every night... every night they would dream."

As she spoke the mocking tone that had previously polluted her words ebbed away, replaced with something more distant.

"They didn't realise for a long time that not everyone dreamt like them, building a shared world of adventure and magic around themselves as they slept, night after night. Instead, they revelled in their abilities and started to spend more and more time in their world of dreams, captivated by the chance to make their adventures real, until eventually they were passing more time playing there than in the world they had been born into."

Adam swallowed, finding it hard not to let the hypnotic lilt of her words carry him along. The things she was saying were altogether too familiar, too close to home.

"But the girl started to worry, she felt that they were slowly losing themselves in this imagined world and decided that she would put an end to her dreaming. She picked a night that would be her last before she said goodbye to it all forever... but then, on that last night, things all went terribly wrong."

Adam saw Ephialtes fingers clench into fists as she spoke, her long nails making an unpleasant rasping noise as they scraped on the stone arms of the throne.

"Every night when they entered their world, they would each take a small memento with them, a trinket that was their key to enter... and to leave. But that night, that last night, when she went to leave for the very last time... her key and that of her brother had both gone. To her surprise her brother wasn't sad or scared; he had grown to love the Dream World more than his own and now that their route home was gone he seemed almost happy. He buried himself in the Dream World completely, but even then, so far from home, eventually he grew tired and found a safe place to sleep. Because he too had lost his key, sleeping didn't send him home as it should have, instead, he stayed in the Dream World and the visions he had as he slept spread slowly all around the world."

To Adam's side, Lucid's struggles had ceased, and from the corner of his eye Adam could see he was now stood completely still, listening intently.

"But unlike her brother, the girl had lost her love for the world she now found herself trapped in. More than anything else she wanted to leave and walk on the streets where she had been born. Rather than give herself over to sleep she searched for her key, searched for years... and then one day she finally found where it was hidden..."

Adam felt that the story was reaching its climax, but instead of finishing her tale Ephialtes paused, distracted and looking over Adam's shoulder.

"Aha," she said. "It looks like my servant has returned. I believe that this is what you were looking for?" The Nightmare that had left so hurriedly earlier shambled past Adam and held one huge hand out flat in front of the Queen, its head bowed and several of its pairs of eyes remaining respectfully downcast. Reaching out daintily, as if plucking a favourite chocolate from a selection box, she picked a small, unmistakably shiny object from off the open palm.

"I believe that this is what you are here for?" she asked, sliding the ring down one long nail and letting it dangle, glinting gently in the half-light.

Adam felt an overwhelming desire to reach out and grab it. Memories of times spent with his mother overwhelmed him, his mind filled with remembered moments from long before he had ever entered Reverie, back when the biggest problems he had to deal with were the horrors of late homework or sleeping slightly later than he planned.

The long, bony fingers snapped closed around the ring like a mousetrap, hiding it from Adam's view and dragging his mind back from the happier times in his memories to the far more unpleasant present. "Not so fast young man," Ephialtes chided. "Your mother has been a thorn in my side for a very long time, and this ring is the closest I have come to holding her beating heart in my hand."

She squeezed her hand tight, staring at Adam as she spoke.

"Fine... fine, what do you want?" he asked, unable to think of anything other than his mum, slowly fading away.

"Good, you are a quick learner," she said. "Everything in this world... in all worlds... has a cost, and the cost for this ring is suitably steep. There is an item that means a lot to me. Something I hold as dear as you hold this ring. Something I have searched for, for many, many years. Something that I finally found and which, to my very great annoyance, I realised I couldn't take back for myself."

She reached out her skinny arm and extended a finger. One long and slightly crooked nail grazed the underneath of Adam's chin, lifting his head slightly so that his eyes were staring straight into hers. "But I believe that you can go where even I cannot. You can enter the Garden and bring me back my music box."

Adam blinked, surprised by both the banality of her request and the momentary flicker of what looked like longing in the Queens otherwise flat and lifeless eyes.

CHAPTER 16

Nora was trying to sleep, but unfortunately sleep was not having any of it. Instead of doing the decent thing and letting Nora get the rest she increasingly needed, sleep was playing hard to get, skipping away just out of reach every time it seemed like she might catch up to it.

Turning uncomfortably from side to side Nora was increasingly convinced that she might as well just give it up as a bad job and get out of bed. "Arrghh... stupid sleep, stupid dreams..." she grumbled to herself, punching her pillow in a vain effort to shape it into something a little more comfortable.

She was so busy taking out her frustrations on the unfortunate pillow that she almost didn't hear the voice that whispered her name, "Nora..."

She froze, mid punch, unsure if she had really heard anything. "I really need to get some sleep," she muttered, "now I'm hearing things."

She was about to resume pummelling the pillow when the voice, more clearly this time, repeated her name. "Nora... Nora..."

She knew she should be scared, hearing mysterious whispering voices was not normally a good sign, but something about the voice, although it was still extremely quiet, was also very familiar.

"Who's there?" she asked, a bit of a tremor in her voice despite her best efforts.

"Finally, I thought you were never going to hear me!" the voice replied, more loudly this time, and with a discordant undertone that Nora was now sure she recognised.

"Mittens?"

"Give the girl a prize... all that time we spent together and now you hardly recognise your old room-mate."

"Mittens... it is you... where have you been?" Nora replied, aware that there was an accusational undertone in her voice.

"Back in Reverie, as you well know," Mittens replied. "Things have been... rather busy since I returned. Life there, especially for the Nightmares is much worse than I remembered..." she tailed off. "Still now is not the time for long explanations, there will be enough time for that later. For the moment I need you to come with me. Your optimistic young friend Adam is in big trouble."

Nora pushed herself upright in her bed, her tiredness immediately vanishing. "What's happened to him?"

"He went to face the Queen of the Nightmares... I even helped him on his way. But now he is walking into the biggest trap in all of Reverie, an ancient Nightmare of such size and artfulness that most no longer even realise what it is. More than ever he needs the help of his friends around him. Your companion is brave and strong... for a flimsy human, but what he faces now is beyond him."

Bristling slightly at the implied criticism Nora snapped back, "I have tried to go to Reverie every night for weeks, but I can't get there. You said that I would be okay, but I haven't, I haven't been okay at all!"

There was a slight shimmering in the air just in front of Nora and when Mittens spoke again her voice was closer, her familiar rasping tones right by Nora's ear.

"I don't know what's stopped you. I can see even now that you have everything you need to enter Reverie... that and more. There must be something else, some inner doubt or fear that holds you back."

"I'm not scared," Nora replied, annoyed at the suggestion.

"Then show me," Mittens' voice taunted her, and as she did Nora felt all the frustration and anger since losing her way into Reverie bubble to the surface and overwhelm her, like a dam finally breaking and releasing a torrent it had been straining to hold back for far, far too long.

She could also feel the start of a strange burning sensation near her hand, and looking down, her vision slightly misted and her head thrumming with tension, she could see the spot where Mittens used to rest around her wrist glowing gently. But instead of seeing the coiled shadow of Mittens there was a paler patch of skin, like a birthmark in exactly the same pattern.

"Told you." The disembodied voice sounded satisfied. "Now we must go. What is that saying you humans have... ah yes, time... and giant nightmare monsters wait for no man."

The new pain in her wrist still flaring, Nora's vision began to spin and fade before finally vanishing into a tiny black pin-prick, but instead of feeling afraid the last sensation she had was one of elation. "Watch out Reverie," she thought to herself before she let herself drop away into the beckoning darkness, "I'm coming back."

CHAPTER 17

"So, what do you think?" Adam asked as he and Lucid made his way along the tunnel Ephialtes had directed them to. "If we find this music-box she was talking about do you reckon she really will return my mum's ring?"

Lucid scowled. He had hardly spoken a word since the Queen had released him from the bands that had wrapped him almost head to foot.

"What I think about that monster is best left unsaid," he replied bitterly. "But I would expect that whatever she wants is no good for us, or anyone except her. So, no... I don't think we can trust her. Not that we have many other options at the moment." He paused to rub his wrists gingerly, still painful so soon after his release. "But the other things she was saying... the story she told us, about the brother and sister who got trapped in Reverie. If that was true it would mean that the Dreamer..."

He stopped, his eyes still troubled. "I need to think..."

The next few minutes passed in silence as they made their way through the cave. The last few metres of the uneven, pitted walls giving way to smooth stone, forming a perfectly arched passage. A distant brightness spilled across the far end of the tunnel, illuminating the stone with a gently wavering light, warm and welcoming after the continuous, heavy darkness of the tunnels.

A few more steps took Adam through the end of the stone passage and as he did the cramped surroundings opened out into a completely unexpected vista.

Blinking a few times to adjust to the sudden brightness Adam took in the vast space he had entered. Rather than rough stone under his feet, there was lush, thick grass, while all around him there was greenery and life. Trees of all shapes and sizes spread out as far as the eye could see, while smaller plants, bursting with life and colour clustered around their trunks. Overhead, rather than the oppressively close stone of a cavern, there was clear blue sky, with birds circling noisily in the thermals.

"How can this exist in the middle of all that... horribleness everywhere around it?" Adam asked, still shocked to see so much greenery and beauty.

"It's the Garden," Lucid replied simply, as if that short sentence was a full description in itself. Then seeing Adam's expression, he began again.

"Sorry... you have spent so much time here that I forget much of this world is still a mystery to you. The Garden is much more than just a simple green space. The Garden is... or was once upon a time, right at the centre of Reverie, some say it was here even before the Stairway of Dreams."

Adam looked around, trying to take in as much of the surroundings as he could. Looking more closely at some of the nearest trees their age was obvious, trunks wide and doughty, canopies extending much higher and wider than any of the trees that Adam could recollect from home.

"But that's not the most important thing you should know about the Garden," Lucid continued. "What everyone knows... or at least everyone that lives in Reverie full time, is that the Garden is where the best dreams happen. It's where dreamers come when they have a perfect dream, one where all their wishes come true. When they can experience true happiness... at least for a while."

Looking across the open green expanse laid out before them Adam tried to spot any wandering dreamers, thinking it would be a nice change to see someone looking happy, rather than running from their Nightmare, but he couldn't see anyone.

"You won't see any dreamers this far out," Lucid told him, displaying once again his uncanny ability to tell what Adam was thinking. "If anything that I've been told is true, if any of the tales are real, then we are still too far away from the centre, from the real Garden."

He pointed off into the distance, to a spot where the trees were clustered most tightly. "I would suspect that's where we need to be. I would, however, point out that it has been a very long time since anyone has ventured into the Garden and... I am not sure what effect it may have on anyone who enters it through choice. There were old stories, but..."

Rather than continuing he struck out towards the thicker tree line on the horizon, long strides quickly eating up the distance.

Adam followed after him as fast as he was able, although he had to maintain an awkward half-jog to keep up with Lucid's longer legs. As they delved further into the Garden, heading towards the centre, Adam could feel the atmosphere changing. Every time his feet touched the ground, he could have sworn that he could feel a glow of wellbeing running up his legs and warming his chest, filling him with energy. Looking across at Lucid he could see that he was experiencing the same sensation, an increasingly wide grin on his face. Both of them were speeding up, breaking into a jog, then a run and finally a sprint, pelting across the thickly grassed meadowlands towards the thick band of trees as fast as they were able.

Normally Adam would have been out of breath by now, the ability to run for more than a few minutes without needing a rest not among his newly found skills in the Dreamworld. But here, in the Garden, it seemed like he could run forever, the ground passing under his feet so fast he almost felt like he was gliding over the surface. He felt oddly disappointed to reach the first of the huge trees that formed a green wall around the very centre of the place, letting the temporary freedom of the mindless dash slip away as he slowed back down to a walk.

"So, this is the real Garden then?" Adam asked, looking around slowly. The band of huge trees was no more than a hundred metres deep, thinning again as they walked through.

"It would seem so," Lucid replied as he walked beside Adam, long fingers outstretched, brushing against the tall ferns that clustered around the tree-trunks. "I have no idea what to expect when we enter the true Garden, I remember that there were stories about this place but..." he faltered momentarily as they broke through the tree line, the returning sunlight washing over them like a warm bath.

The sight that had opened out in front of them was unbelievably beautiful, lush greenery as far as the eye could see. Thick grass cushioned Adam's steps and all around there were clusters of plants and flowers, all bursting with life, colour, and vitality. At first sight, the groupings of plants appeared random, but the more Adam looked the more it seemed that there was a subtle underlying pattern, that they were markers, guiding him further towards the very centre.

His thoughts were disturbed for a moment by the shrill cry somewhere high above, and looking up, he spotted a circling group of brightly plumed birds basking lazily in the warm air. When he looked down again, he realised that Lucid was no longer beside him, presumably off exploring the garden.

A quiet voice, tickling at the back of his brain, wondered how Lucid had managed to slip away so quickly, but before he could give the thought too much attention Adam was distracted by a voice coming from somewhere just ahead, a voice calling out his name.

"Adam..."

Peering into the distance he tried to see who had called, but it sounded like the voice had come from within a copse of smaller trees a little way ahead of him, each one of them dotted with brightly coloured blossoms.

As he drew close his name was called out again, and this time he could hear it more clearly, the voice familiar, immediately bringing a lump to his throat.

"Mum?"

He couldn't tell exactly where the voice was coming from, but from somewhere behind the thick cluster of trees, low branches blocking his view, there was a gently glowing light.

"Just a little further Adam, you are nearly there. All you need to do is find what the Queen wants and then we can be together again, a family like before."

At the back of his mind, a tiny but determined voice that he recognised as his own was grumbling away, trying to make itself heard, but Adam wasn't interested in anything it had to say. This was it, the moment he had been waiting for so long, the chance to save his mum... and he wasn't about to let some stupid chatter inside his own head spoil it for him.

"Fine," his inner voice said, "be like that, but don't say I didn't warn you... because I did."

And with that, the inside of his head fell quiet, although he could still feel the irritating tickle of discontent lurking somewhere in there.

He pushed aside the last of the low branches blocking his view, impatient to see what they had been hiding. The view he was treated to didn't disappoint. If the rest of the garden had been an example of the lushest greenery Adam had ever seen, the clearing he had entered was beyond anything he could have imagined. The stem of every plant was at the perfect angle to catch the sunlight on the spots of dew dotted along its length, glistening like tiny diamonds, each individual petal was a work of art.

The whole place reeked of health and life, so strong that Adam could almost swear he could feel a giant heartbeat slowly thudding through his feet, lifting his spirits even further.

Right in the very centre of the final clearing was a small, shallow lake, and in the middle of that was a small rocky mass rising out of the water. From a distance, it looked like there could be some sort of opening in the rock, and it was from there that Adam was convinced his mother's voice was coming.

As he drew closer, he could see that resting on the uneven ledges of stone that circled the rocky growth there were a number of small trinkets, surprisingly plain looking amongst all the natural wonders of the garden. Without realising how he'd got there, Adam found himself wading through the water towards them.

"That's it Adam, you're nearly there," his mum's voice echoed gently. He tried to speed up, but he was finding it surprisingly hard to make his way through the water. Despite the fact that it only came up to his ankles it was heavy going, feeling more like forcing his way through treacle.

"That's pretty weird don't you think," his inner voice piped up, sensing a chance to make itself heard again.

"Shut up," he told himself.

"But you've got to admit it's a bit strange," inner Adam persisted. "I am pretty sure that water isn't supposed to cling to your clothes like that. And isn't it a bit odd that your mum's voice is coming from somewhere in the Garden, when I am pretty sure we left her back with Mittens. If you ask me..."

"I am not asking you," Adam snapped back, stubbornly determined not to look down at the water still dragging rather unpleasantly at his ankles.

"Can't help some people... especially when that person is you... or me... or whatever..." his inner voice replied, before dropping into sulky silence again.

Without the disturbance inside his head holding him back, Adam managed to wade through the last few metres of the shallow lake, relieved to reach the stony area. As he had thought there was an opening in the rock face, and now he was close enough to see it clearly it looked like it was indeed a cave of some sort. Although it was fairly murky and dark, there were a series of roughly hewn steps within the rock of the cave leading downwards, which Adam presumed meant there could be a larger cavern somewhere under the lake.

As he reached out to grasp the edge of the opening and pull himself out of the water he was shocked at how warm the surface of the rock felt to the touch. As he gasped at the sudden heat he drew in a deep involuntary breath, drawing back his hand in surprise. A moment later he was doubled over, gagging at the rotten taste in his mouth. The deep breath of air he had taken in was rancid, tasting of dank, dark rot, a world away from the beautiful surroundings.

For a moment Adam was pretty sure he heard a quiet, but very smug, "told you..." from deep within his own head, but then his inner voice was drowned out by another that he knew every bit as well as his own.

"Well done Adam, you're doing so well. Don't give up now. Just a few more steps and we will be able to go home... safe... together. That's what you want isn't it?"

"Okay mum," Adam managed to croak, straightening himself up and taking another deep breath. This one didn't leave any sort of bad taste, in fact, it had the opposite effect, filling Adam with a sense of purpose. His doubts vanished, and he took his first step into the cave, so focused on reaching his goal that he didn't immediately hear the sudden flurry of noise over his shoulder. By the time he had realised that there was someone or something behind him, it was much too late. There was a sudden pain in the back of his head, and he slumped forward.

Although he didn't lose consciousness completely, everything around him was confused, his vision swimming in and out of focus. He could feel himself being lifted and there was a sensation of movement. This was followed by the feeling of something warm under him and then the sound of air rushing past his ears. Blinking uncomfortably, with his eyes stinging and a dull and unpleasant ache still in the back of his head, he could feel some sensation beginning to return to his arms and legs. As his vision settled, he was greeted with the unexpected sight of Nora staring down at him.

Fairly convinced he must be dreaming, which even in his confused state he realised was either highly unlikely or ridiculously ironic, (considering where he was), he stared back at her blankly.

"Seriously, what were you thinking?" she asked him despairingly. "I have only been away from Reverie for a few weeks and look at all the trouble you've managed to get yourself into."

Adam tried to form a few words in his defence but was still feeling far too groggy and only managed a semi-coherent grunt, which didn't seem to achieve much.

As feeling continued to return to the rest of his body Adam was increasingly aware of an uncomfortable flexing sensation under his back and a definite feeling of movement. He tried to push himself up into a seated position, and as he did everything around him slotted into place. The flexing he could feel was the rolling movement of two large, strong shoulder-blades directly under his back. The sense of motion was as a result of the fact that he, or whatever he was on, was definitely moving. And by the look of the clouds that were whipping past, moving extremely fast.

His brain finally also caught onto the fact that clouds were not normally something you could see quite so closely, and that, in combination with the rush of air that he could still feel across his face, meant only one thing.

Nora grinned at him. "I wouldn't look down if I were you."

Of course this meant that was the very first thing he did, twisting himself over from his back and then immediately wishing he hadn't. For a start, the back of the creature he was lying on wasn't particularly broad, and for a moment one of his arms had flailed out into the open air. Secondly, they were a long, long way from the ground, the lush green of the garden far beneath him.

"What... how...?" Adam managed, pushing himself up into a seated position and letting his legs straddle the back of... whatever it was he was on. The creature beneath him looked a lot like a horse, but on a larger scale, it's back strong enough to carry both him and Nora. The long, dark mane whipped in the wind and to either side were huge sinuous wings, slowly beating in time with the flex of its shoulders.

"This is one of the Mara?" he asked, thinking back to the Nightmare beasts in the huge underground stables. "I thought that they were only used by the Queen of the Nightmares... and that they eat people."

"No idea, but they seem to quite like me," Nora told him, having to shout to be heard above the wind.

"It's great to see you... but how are you even here? I thought you couldn't get back into Reverie?"

"I managed to get in touch with my inner Mittens... with a little bit of help," Nora replied, and as she did a dark film briefly rippled across her eyes. "And it was her... Mittens that told me that you needed help, that you were about to do something really, really stupid."

Recent memories came flooding back, filling Adam's head. He remembered the Garden, the voice of his mother and the siren call from the cave in the centre of the lake. He had been so incredibly close, and then something... or someone had knocked him out before he could reach his goal.

"Was that you?" he asked angrily. "You that hit me. You stopped me from getting what I needed to save my mum."

"Yes," Nora replied, not looking in the least sorry. "You're welcome by the way." Reaching into her pocket she pulled out a small music box and showed it to him. "This is what you were after. You walked straight past it on your way into that creature's mouth."

"What?" Adam asked, increasingly confused, his brief moment of annoyance sputtering out as quickly as it had started.

"Didn't you think there was something odd about the garden?" Nora asked him. "Didn't it seem too perfect, too eager to give you exactly what you wanted? If you had gone into the cave, you would have never, ever have come out again... look..."

She pointed down below them, and following the line of her finger, Adam could see the cave and the shallow lake far below them. It was odd, from this height the garden looked rather less pretty, and even more strangely it looked like the surface of the garden was moving slightly. He tried to remember what he had seen in the cave. Admittedly his brain had been a bit foggy at the time, but there had been a slightly strange smell coming from somewhere within the rock. Thinking back with a clearer head, the rocky outcrops within the cave had also been quite pointy, almost like massive teeth... but that was ridiculous.

"What on earth?"

"Mittens told me all about it," Nora said. "The Garden isn't what it appears to be. It's one giant trap, the greatest and most ancient Nightmare in all of Reverie, passing itself off as the most beautiful dream you have ever wished for. It offers you whatever it is you want the most in the world and lures you right to the centre. That's where it lives, right in the middle of the Garden. Like a massive spider sitting in the centre of its web, it waits for its prey to walk willingly into its mouth."

Adam gulped, what Nora was saying sounded crazy, but it also made a strange kind of sense, especially now he was clear of the Garden and the strange tricks it had been playing with his brain. From this height the bands of trees that he had walked through looked more structured and organised than he had realised, guiding you slowly but inevitably towards the centre.

"Lucid!" Adam gasped, he had nearly forgotten that his friend had entered the Garden with him. "Where is Lucid. We can't leave him down there."

"He's fine, look," Nora pointed across to the side, and there weaving through the clouds was another of the giant, flying horses. Clinging to its back, eyes squeezed firmly closed, was Grimble and seated directly behind him, raising his top hat in welcome, was the unmistakable figure of Lucid.

Adam was about to wave back, relieved to see his friends safe and well, when the Mara carrying them suddenly gave a startled whinny and veered sharply to one side. A split second later and a lump of flying rock shot through the spot they had occupied just moments before.

Desperately looking around to see where the sudden attack had come from, Adam saw that the surface of the garden was more than rippling, it was moving, sections tearing free, flinging shards of stone and chunks of earth violently into the air as it did so. The outcrop in the lake was right in the centre of the heaving mass, and as Adam watched with increasing horror the whole section rose slowly skywards, the surrounding land collapsing around it.

What emerged from the ground was unimaginably huge, grotesque and horrifying in equal measure. The cave that Adam had so nearly walked straight into had split wide open, revealing what looked like a massive and very unpleasant tongue. Underneath this was a tall and gangly body, wrapped in dark red sinews, looking like the roots of a particularly nasty weed, dragging itself angrily from the ground.

"Ughhh," Adam grunted, "I nearly ended up in the mouth of that... thing."

"Told you," Nora replied grimly. "We only just reached you in time, but it doesn't look like we're safe yet."

The Mara they were riding gave a violent jerk to one side as another shard of rock came screaming through the air, passing within a few metres of them. Adam nearly lost his seat and shouting an apology to the steed below, gripped a handful of the creature's mane as tightly as he could.

Nora had wrapped her arms tightly around his chest and was holding on with equal determination. "Come on," she shouted, "we need to get out of its reach as fast as we can." Another flying object came whistling through the air, this time looking like half of one the tall trees that Adam had admired just a few minutes ago.

Squeezing his eyes closed, trying to block out all the surrounding chaos, Adam tried to think of a Daydream that would help but the task seemed impossible. The creature roaring furiously below them was the size of a skyscraper. Rather than a specific dream, he thought back to the times before when he had protected Nora, first in the middle of Isenbard's Horror and then again in the collapsing Chimera facility in Moonshine. Unfortunately, both times he had reacted without really thinking about what he was doing, which was not all that helpful now.

The Mara carrying them swerved violently once again, as yet another huge trunk of a half-destroyed tree flew past, this time so close that Adam could see every detail of the shattered tree, shards of wood sticking out at awkward angles where it had been torn apart by the huge Nightmare. Behind him Nora tensed, giving a small inhalation of fear. This seemed to spur his imagination, giving it the kick-start it needed, and a moment later he felt his mind wrap itself around the flying trunk, before catapulting it back down towards the monster below them. It wasn't exactly what he had intended, but once again it seemed his brain had stepped in to help him without really knowing what he was doing.

Whether it was beginner's luck, or he had discovered a previously undiscovered skill at throwing trees, his aim was perfect and the giant shard of wood crashed directly into the giant creatures upturned face. As it stumbled back unsteadily on its long, spindly limbs it lost its footing and with an ominous creaking sound it dropped ponderously backward into the shallow waters of the lake, creating a huge, rippling tidal-wave.

"Not bad," Nora muttered. "Glad to see that you haven't completely lost it."

"Um... thanks," Adam replied, deciding he would take her comment as a compliment, regardless of how it may have been intended. "Do you know the way back to the Queen's chamber? I need to get the music box back to her as soon as I can. My mum needs something that the Queen has, and I don't think that there is much time." He stopped, looking back across at the other Mara, with Lucid and Grimble perched uncomfortably on its back.

"What's Grimble doing here?" Adam asked, "Last time I saw him, he said he was going to stay with my mum and look after her."

"Don't worry," Nora told him, with a reassuring squeeze. "Your mum is fine. She is pretty much the first person I saw when I got back into Reverie. She's really nice by the way... although she was pretty mad at you for having run off."

Adam breathed a sigh of relief. He didn't care that his mum was angry with him, he didn't care if she was going to shout, he didn't even care if she was going to tell him she was 'disappointed.' All that mattered was that she was still okay, and now they had the music box that the Queen was so desperate for, they were a big step closer to getting his mum home safely.

"So now what?" Nora asked.

"Now I take this back to the Queen, I get my mums ring and we all go home," said Adam firmly, with a lot more confidence than he felt. Deep down his misgivings about the Queen and the chances of her honouring the deal were growing stronger by the second. He could feel the glow of his pendant burning gently against his chest, but he had no idea whether this was in celebration or warning.

CHAPTER 18

It was not much more than an hour later when Adam found himself back in the throne room, but this time with the Queen's music box clasped firmly in hand. He knew he probably looked a bit of a state, battered and bruised by his experiences in the Garden, but he didn't particularly care. Instead, the whole thing had left him more determined than ever. This time he returned the glares of the Nightmares that flanked his approach to the throne with an even more menacing stare of his own. It didn't seem to have much effect on them, but it made him feel better, so he continued to glare at every Nightmare monster that looked his way for the entire, uncomfortable walk.

Lucid was alongside him once again, but Grimble and Nora had stayed hidden back in the next cavern, amongst the stabled Mara. Explaining their presence would have been far too complicated for Adam's tired brain, plus he had a sneaking suspicion that Grimble, and quite possibly Nora, would end up saying something that would upset the Queen... probably a lot.

As they drew close, Adam could see Ephialtes looking down at him with a fascinated look on her bony features

"I bet you are surprised", Adam thought to himself bitterly. "By now I could easily have been in the belly of that massive Nightmare."

"Welcome back Daydreamer," the Queen greeted him, managing to sound almost welcoming. "I hear that you were successful, that you have found that which I had lost for so very long."

"We found your box," Adam replied, trying his best to keep his voice neutral, "and I will give it to you... once I have my mother's ring like you promised."

Ephialtes sighed. "It is a shame that you can't be more trusting young man... but if that is what you want."

One of the Nightmares stood close to the throne reached up and handed a small box to her, which the Queen took and tossed up and down in one hand thoughtfully.

"I went to a lot of trouble to get this ring," she said quietly. "I hope that you won't disappoint me." Then with a final flick of her long fingers, she sent the box spinning across to Adam who caught it awkwardly.

Not wasting any time, he lifted the lid and there, securely nestled in the box, was a small, tacky looking ring that he recognised all too well.

"Is that it?" Lucid muttered across to him. "Is that your mother's ring?"

Adam nodded. He knew with unwavering certainty that this was what he had been looking for. It was a strange feeling, but looking at the ring he could almost see his mum's face reflected in the surface of the replica gemstone smiling back at him.

Lucid reached inside his frockcoat and pulled out the small, rectangular shape of the music box and handed it to Adam.

"Here," Adam said, giving the box to the same Nightmare who had been sent to collect his mother's ring. It had a particularly unsettling selection of spines all the way around its face, which Adam took to be an odd and unpleasant sign of seniority.

The Nightmare shuffled between Adam and the throne, handing the music box across while managing to keep all eight of its eyes respectfully averted from the Queen.

"Finally," Ephialtes sighed as she stared hungrily at the tiny, decorated box perched on the stretched parchment of her hand.

Using one long nail she unclipped the small metal clasp that held the lid closed, tipping the lid back, and a miniature ballerina sprang up, slowly rotating as a tinny tune began to play in time with her shaky rotations.

The room descended into silence as the Queen sat transfixed, never taking her eyes from the revolving figure. Then, inevitably the clockwork which had been powering the box's crude mechanism wound down and the slow dance came to an end, the last few metallic notes slow and uneven.

Shaking herself free of whatever old avenue of thought she had been travelling down the Queen looked back up at Adam. Her eyes, which had previously been as hollow as the deep sockets that surrounded them, were shining with a new light.

"I must thank you, young man," she said, placing the music box down on one of the stone arms of the throne before rising to her feet. "This box, this little trinket of my youth, means more than you could ever imagine. Without it I could never go home, never realise my full potential."

Trying to ignore the cold, sick feeling that was rapidly working its way up from his stomach, Adam faced her as she towered over him, seeming even taller and more gaunt than before, as she continued to speak.

"I have dreamt for so long of what I would do when I finally got it back... and now I have it the first thing I will do is take down that accursed stairway, end the dream that you all seem to think is the key to the creation of this world."

As she spoke, the gestures that accompanied her speech became broader and more violent.

"You will see soon enough that the Dreamer didn't create this world, he merely shaped it. Without his influence, I will finally have my chance to show you the way the world could be. And then... then I will return home... and what a glorious homecoming that will be."

As she finished she raised both arms above her, fists clenched, and the crowds of Nightmares erupted in a cacophony of whoops, roars and growls.

"I think we may have made a bit of a mistake," Lucid muttered out the side of his mouth to Adam. "We have just given the keys of the world to a madwoman."

"For the minute let's just get this ring back to my mum," Adam said, struggling to make himself heard over the roars of the surrounding Nightmares. "We can try and work out what to do after that."

He began to slowly back away from the throne, with Lucid staying close alongside him, but quickly realised that the gap in the gathered crowds that they had used to approach the throne had been closed off, with the throng of Nightmares now completely surrounding them.

"Where do you think you are going Daydreamer?" the Queen asked, descending from the throne's raised dais with slow, deliberate steps, the black gossamer of her gown cascading behind her.

"We got you what you wanted," Adam replied, fighting the temptation to back away even further, which was helped by the fact that he couldn't have even if he tried, the nearest Nightmares pressing uncomfortably close behind him.

"You did... and I am grateful, but I am afraid that if I allowed you to leave, and to return that ring to your troublesome mother, that you would both continue to be... inconvenient. That is something that I just can't accept. Reverie is changing, and there will be no place in the world for Daydreamers."

Ephilates reached out and ran one long, sharp nail across several outstretched strands of her lank, dark hair. One after another they drifted towards the ground, where they shimmered and writhed before each one slowly expanded, growing into the misshapen

171

figures that Adam recognised all too well from their clash on the circus ship.

"So that's where they come from," Lucid muttered incredulously.

"That's pretty weird... and kind of disgusting."

"Take him," the Queen instructed, and one after another the squat shapeless figures turned towards Adam, shifting between individual stilted movements like a cheap animation.

"I knew it," Adam grumbled to himself, which was no particular comfort and equally little use, as the menacing figures drew slowly but inexorably closer. "I knew that she couldn't be trusted."

"Which makes you the idiot," his traitorous, but he had to accept, probably correct, inner voice added. "Still, let's not make it easy for her."

"I agree," Adam replied (to himself), although this time he said it out loud, drawing a confused look from Lucid, who was standing close to one side, eyes darting back and forth between Adam and the approaching monsters.

"Any thoughts?" Lucid asked, in a completely unsuccessful attempt to sound cool and calm.

Sucking in a deep inward breath, Adam tried to focus his mind and summon a Daydream that would help. He found himself missing the strange, fizzing potions and gadgets that Grimble always seemed to be able to dig out in an emergency. But he knew that Grimble was too far away to help, so instead his mind flashed back to the giant crashing pillar that the Nightmares had been using in the mine, and the thought gave him a moment of inspiration.

"Stay close by my side," he told Lucid and then, concentrating as hard as he could he raised one hand into the air, stretched high above his head before bringing it crashing down towards the hard, rocky floor underfoot.

Clenching his fist as tightly as he could, he willed it to become something much more solid and much, much heavier. He could feel the familiar warm glow of the pendant around his neck and at the same time a strange sensation running down his arm, like pins and needles multiplied a hundred times over. By the time his hand reached the ground, it had changed completely, made of the same hard rock as the pillar that had repeatedly split open the ground of the mines. When his hand made contact with the floor, the energy of something much larger transferred through the relatively small area of his fist, the result was explosive. A huge shockwave rippled across the floor of the cavern, sending Nightmares tumbling across the room, knocking into each other, tripping each other up and generally causing carnage. Lucid had also lost his footing, but Adam gripped him by the shoulder and helped him straight back onto his feet, pointing at the exit where Grimble and Nora were still hidden.

"Come on!" he shouted over the mass of background roars, rumblings, and shrieks that surrounded them. With that, he and Lucid started running, as fast they were able on the unstable ground.

They made surprisingly good progress, considering that the cavern seemed to contain pretty much every unpleasant Nightmare creature that Adam could imagine (and quite a few he wouldn't have been able to imagine even if he tried really hard). The uproar caused by Adam's minor earthquake meant that they made it nearly three-quarters of the way to the exit before they ran into any serious problems.

This far from the centre of the chamber the effects had been less extreme, and several of the larger Nightmares had got themselves organised enough to block Adam and Lucid's route. In the middle of the cluster, a good head height taller than the others was a particularly terrifying, yet familiar looking monster. One of his catlike eyes winked, or at least Adam presumed it was a wink, with the eyelids closing side to side rather than top to bottom, then it reached out to either side with huge, sinewy arms and banged the heads of the two closest other Nightmares together, knocking them to the ground.

Without pausing Adam and Lucid ran through the temporary gap that their unexpected friend had provided. As they sprinted past Adam was pretty sure that he saw it make the sign of the 'Triple F' with one massive hand.

"Thank you!" Adam shouted over his shoulder, and the creature smiled back before vanishing under a mass of other Nightmares, several of the short, shadowy figures of the Queen's new creations amongst them.

Ahead of them, Adam could see Nora and Grimble emerging from behind the rocks where they had been hiding. Nora was lashing out with long dark tendrils that took several more of the Nightmares from their feet, while Grimble shook a small vial before throwing it into the mass of monsters, spraying a sticky web-like substance over several of them. It set solid in seconds leaving them looking like a series of extremely lifelike, and very angry, gargoyles.

For a minute it seemed that they were going to make it out of the cavern, the safety of the tunnel only metres away, but as Adam took the last few steps he felt his movements slow, a terrible cold sensation washing over his body, freezing his muscles. He could see Nora looking at something just over his shoulder, a look of horror on her face. Involuntarily he turned to see what had got her attention and there, just behind him were several of the squat figures of the Queen's Nightmares, stood in a cluster with a deep black portal massing behind them.

He could feel the pull of the shadows, drawing him in, away from his friends and the tantalisingly close prospect of freedom. The edges of his vision shimmered with encroaching darkness and he knew with a hard, painful certainty that he only had seconds left before he was taken completely. Nora and Grimble had fought their way to him and started desperately but hopelessly pulling at his arms.

"Take this," Adam managed, pressing his mother's ring into the palm of Nora's hand so hard that it hurt. "Give it to my mum, she needs this, it will save her..."

Then his grip loosened, and he vanished back into the swirling nightmare darkness.

The last view Nora had of him was his outstretched fingers, still reaching out for her hand, disappearing into the black void. For a moment she just stood there, too shell-shocked to do, or even think anything. Stumbling backward she felt strong hands grip her by the shoulders, steadying her before she fell. "We have to go...." Turning she looked to see Lucid's face, tight with emotion, his voice cracking as he spoke. "We have to go right now."

"But... Adam..." she said, her words coming out as a whisper, "we can't just leave him."

"We can... and we must," Lucid replied, "he risked everything to get that ring back. Now it's up to us to get it back to his mother. With one final pull on her arm, he dragged her back into the tunnel entrance, where Grimble was fiddling with a tightly bundled package.

"Five seconds!" he shouted to them both as they staggered past him, the mass of approaching Nightmares only a few metres away from the tunnel.

"What?"

"Three seconds now... in fact two... argh, just run!" Grimble yelled, taking his own advice and passing both Lucid and Nora with an impressive turn of speed, short arms and legs pumping. A moment later there was a huge bang, as whatever Grimble had prepared exploded into life, collapsing the rocky entrance to the tunnel closed behind them.

CHAPTER 19

Nora paid little attention to their journey back through the caves and tunnels, letting either Lucid or Grimble lead the way, occasionally reaching out to steer her by the shoulder with a kindly hand as she stumbled blindly onwards. The last few moments with Adam played over and over in her head, the look on his face as he vanished backwards into the darkness burned clearly into her brain. She was still clutching the ring tightly in her right hand, refusing to put it away in a pocket or pass it to one of the others, as if holding onto it tightly enough would somehow bring Adam back.

After what seemed like an eternity, they arrived back at the Triple F's strange sitting room, where Mittens and Adam's mother were both waiting for them.

When Nora, Lucid and Grimble entered the room Adam's mum sprang to her feet, a relieved smile spreading across her face, her eyes darting between the three of them and then looking back over their shoulders, searching for Adam.

When no one else joined them, her smile dropped away and the movement of her eyes became more erratic, constantly flicking between the three of them as if she had somehow managed to miss Adam stood amongst them.

"Where is he... where is Adam?" When she finally spoke, her voice was weak, the words caught up between suddenly heavy and uneven breaths.

"I'm sorry," Lucid replied, his words strained, sounding like they were coming from a long way away, only just managing to finish the painful journey from his brain to his mouth. "He was incredibly brave, but the shadow creatures took him, sucked him away into one of their portals... we were so close..."

He collapsed heavily into one of the oversized seats as he finished speaking, the energy that had somehow been keeping him moving up until that point finally exhausted.

"He did it though, he got your ring back," Nora said, holding out her hand and letting her fingers drop open to the reveal the gaudy trinket, an impression of the fake gemstone left deep in her hand. "It was the last thing he did before they took him, passing me this. He wanted to make sure you got it back, he said it would save you."

Adam's mum was still standing frozen, staring at Nora so blankly that Nora wondered if she had heard a single thing that she had told her. Then she shook her head and gave a short, bitter laugh. "I told him not to go," she said. "I told him it was too dangerous... I should have known he wouldn't listen... I wouldn't have, so I can't blame him."

Slowly she sank into another of the massive armchairs next to Lucid and lifted up her arm so that her hand was directly under the light. Where the light caught it, rather than reflecting off her skin Nora could see straight through to the table below.

"Sadly, whatever it is that is making me fade has started to spread," Adam's mum told them. "Grimble's lotions helped to slow it for a while, but it has come back and nothing seems to be able to stall its progress now."

She turned back to Nora. "The worst of it is that even though you have my ring, after everything that you have all been through, that Adam has been through..." As she spoke his name the words got caught in her throat for a moment and she had to stop speaking, taking a minute to gather herself before continuing. "After all of that, the ring is useless to me here."

She reached out her hand towards Nora, the little finger that had worn the ring extended. The mark around it from years of wearing the cheap band still clear. In return, Nora held out the ring between fingers that had suddenly become clammy with sweat and tried to place it on the extended finger.

To her shock, the ring passed straight through, as did the rest of her hand when she tried to hold the finger steady and try the ring again.

"You see," Adam's mum whispered, it's too far gone. There isn't enough of me left here to wear it. "It was all for nothing. My boy is lost... for nothing. I should never have told him about the ring. I put the thought in his head... it's my fault he's gone."

Nora had no words as she watched Adam's mother lean forward, rest her head in her hands, and begin to rock gently in the seat, a steady trickle of silent tears slipping through the gaps between her fingers.

Nora's hand was stretched halfway out to offer some sort of hopeless comfort when she felt a sudden grip on her shoulder, turning to see Grimble's scowling face.

"Come with me," he grunted, signalling to the other side of the room.

"What do you want?" Nora asked as they reached the far end of the table, some distance from the spot where Lucid and Adam's mother were both seated. "Don't you think it would be better to stay with Adam's mum, she needs people around her at the moment."

"What I think she needs, even more, is for people to think with their heads, not their fuzzy hearts," Grimble replied. He looked up at Nora's horrified expression. "Don't give me that look, I'm every bit as worried about Adam as the rest of you... it's just I haven't let that worry switch the rest of my brain off."

He reached out to grasp Nora's arms with strong, gnarled hands. "The best chance to get Adam back is to have a full-strength Daydreamer on our side, and that Daydreamer is his mother."

"But..." Nora began.

"No buts," Grimble snapped. "There is no time for buts, or what's, or ifs, or maybes. What we do need is for someone, by which I mean you, to go back into the Waking World and get the ring to Adam's mother that way instead. She might be fading away here, but in your world, she will still be able to wear the ring. She will be very weak but it's our best, and most probably only, chance."

Looking down at his grizzled, scarred face Nora was pretty sure for the tiniest of moments that there were the tell-tale glistening marks of tears amongst the grey hair of his face.

"Fine," she replied, deciding it best not to mention it, but strangely reassured that even Grimble wasn't immune to the emotion they were all feeling. "What do you suggest I do."

"You go back, you go back straight away. You find Adam's mum and you make sure that ring goes back on her finger. While I was looking after her she told me whereabouts in your world she has been hiding, so I suggest you go there and do what needs to be done. Are you ready?"

"I suppose so," Nora replied, "but how do I get there, I don't exactly know how this thing I can do works yet. It might take me ages."

Grimble beckoned her to come closer and told her an address that obviously meant nothing to him but was one that she recognised, not particularly far from where she lived. While she was still mulling it over in her head, trying to decide what to do next, he pulled a small paper vial from his pocket, and before she could do anything, he blew heavily, spraying a cloud of fine dust straight into her face.

"What did you... do that... for," she managed before her legs turned to jelly and she sank to the ground. Seconds later and the sights and sounds of Reverie spiralled away.

CHAPTER 20

Waking with a rushed inward gasp of breath, Nora jerked upright. The last few moments in Reverie ricocheting around in her brain. She knew what she had to do and where she had to go, but almost immediately doubts started to eat their way into her. Would she have enough time... what if she failed.

"You need to move yourself," a familiar voice rasped.

"Mittens?"

"Not exactly," the voice replied, "just a little piece of me, probably easiest to think of this as a memory that has stayed with you. Just enough to remind you of what you are capable of... now get moving."

Stopping just long enough to push her feet into her oldest but most comfortable, trainers, Nora dashed past her startled looking mum, out the front door and down the road.

She was halfway down the next street before she remembered it was Monday, and as she turned the corner at the end of the road, she also realised it was the day of the long-awaited maths exam.

By the time she reached the roundabout that led away from the housing estate where she lived and towards the nearby industrial area, she had decided that she didn't care, she would just have to deal with the consequences when all this was over.

She was so busy thinking all of this through that she didn't notice the small patch of shadow that seemed to jump between the reflections in the windows of the parked cars that lined one side of the road, keeping pace with her as she ran.

A few years ago, a local entrepreneur had taken a chance with a rundown patch of old wasteland and managed to build a handful of small industrial units right on the edge of town. Unfortunately for them there hadn't been the demand they had expected, located so far from the motorway, and rather than becoming a thriving centre of commerce the place had slowly deteriorated until just one of the buildings was occupied, and that was by a highly suspect company that claimed to make the world's greatest ice-cream. Judging from how run-down their factory looked, with the sign hanging slightly askew and with metal grills over windows crazed with a network of cracks and chips, it seemed that the rest of the world didn't fully agree with that bold claim.

"Over there," the voice in her head growled, and Nora looked down the estate road, past the ice-cream factory to the next unit along. This building was even more grubby looking, with a heavy metal grate over the door as well as the windows.

"Now what do I do?" Nora muttered to herself, working her way around the building, trying to find a way in. Every window was heavily shuttered and when she tried pulling at one of the metal gratings around the back of the building, safely away from prying eyes, all she achieved was a small painful cut on one of her fingers.

Nora glared at the shutter, sucking on her finger and hoping that the metal covers were more hygienic than they looked. The next moment the shutter crumpled in on itself, turning in seconds from a sheet of substantial looking metal, punched through with a few small holes, to a crumpled mess, no bigger than a snowball. Wrapped tightly around the crushed metal was a long, sinuous shadowy tendril that looked remarkably familiar.

"What on earth," Nora began, looking around to see what could have done this. Then she looked down with a sense of inevitable foreboding, the other end of the coiling shadow was wrapped around her left hand, disappearing seamlessly into a spot just above her wrist. With a gasp she pulled her hand back, trying to pull it clear of the tendril, but all that achieved was to drag the crushed shutter towards her own head. She ducked out of the way just in time as it flew past and crashed into the fence behind her, also leaving a gaping hole where one of the unit's windows had previously been.

The shadowy limb flickered and then dissipated, the last few remnants hanging for a moment around her hand before also disappearing, fading like old smoke. Nora tried to shake her head clear of the unreality of it all. She knew that when Mittens had been with her during their adventures in Moonshine they had done very similar things, but it had always been Mittens who had made it happen, Nora had been nothing more than an observer. This time it had felt different. She was fairly sure, despite not knowing how, that she had done this herself.

Giving her hand one last suspicious look, daring it to try anything else weird or otherworldly, Nora heaved herself up through the newly made opening in the wall and dropped rather heavily into the room on the other side.

Inside the building didn't look quite as bad, although it was a bit sad looking. The shaft of light from the opening Nora had inadvertently made illuminating a small office in the corner of the building, empty other than a plain, functional looking desk. Nora tried flicking the light switch in the corner of the room and wasn't in the least surprised when absolutely nothing happened.

The door between the office and the rest of the building was glazed, but the remainder of the unit was so dark that she couldn't really see anything through the window, and in her rush to leave home she hadn't thought to bring anything like a torch with her. She patted her pockets quickly and realised that she had at least brought her phone. Its light was pretty weak, but it was better than nothing, so swinging it back and forth in front of her like a talisman, lighting up as much of the route ahead as she could with each sweep, she pushed open the connecting door and made her way into the main building.

It looked like the place had been a small factory of some kind, with various bits of large, heavy looking machinery spread out like unpopular exhibits in a really boring museum. Squinting, Nora was surprised to find her night vision improving rapidly in the darkness. Where she had previously only been able to make out the rough shape of each lump of equipment when the light from her phone had briefly danced across it, now she could clearly see the whole of the factory floor. Switching her phone off and stowing it back in her pocket seemed to make no real difference, her eyesight adapting so well that she could now see all the way to the far wall. There was another door, almost exactly opposite her, with a large red and white sign proudly stating that it led the way to 'Storage' of some kind.

There didn't seem to be anything else in this part of the building, so Nora struck out for the far wall, weaving her way between the dormant machines. She was about halfway there when a warning tickled the back of her brain, whispering 'duck!'

Reacting without really thinking, she did what the warning suggested, and a split second later one long metal arm from the nearest piece of equipment swung heavily through the air, exactly where her head had been just moments before. Even then it was still close enough for the particles of displaced dust to irritate Nora's eyes and make her give a short, involuntary sneeze.

"Bless you," said a drawling, familiar and completely unwelcome voice. There was a brief fizzing and humming noise and then the surrounding room began to thrum with activity as machine after machine came to life, operating consoles blinking, conveyor belts whirring and pistons pumping. There was a final plinking sound, and the main lights of the building spluttered into life, bathing the tall figure stood directly in the centre of the room in light.

Tall, strongly built and with long, slightly unkempt blonde hair, his ready smile was every bit as self-satisfied as the last time Nora had seen him.

"Isenbard," she muttered to herself, trying to bite down on the sudden rush of nausea that threatened to overwhelm her. A lot had changed since she had last been face to face with the man who had dragged her into Reverie in the first place, trapping her in a never-ending Nightmare as part of his failed plan to rip the Dream World apart.

She had come a long way from the confused and scared girl that had first been trapped in the Horror. Now she understood the Dream World, and with the help of Mittens, she had realised just what she was capable of. She had faced down Chimera and saved Adam from the clutches of the world's most ancient Nightmare, and yet the sight of Isenbard's smiling face filled her with a cold dread that she could feel running through her veins, freezing up her muscles and tightening her chest with panic.

"It was good of you to lead me here," he drawled. "I have waited a very long time to find Adam's mother. She hid herself away from me extremely well. But now I have found her... and I have you to thank." His smile widened unpleasantly, and he flexed his broad shoulders. "So, if you will excuse me, I have some long unfinished business to conclude." Clicking his fingers casually, he pointed to a filing cabinet on the far wall. As he did the three drawers rumbled for a moment and then shot out, one after another, flying across the room towards Nora.

"Snap out of it!" the rasping voice in her head shouted, shaking her out of her panicked state. Diving to one side she narrowly avoided the first of the drawers, which crashed into the machinery just behind her, spraying the air with scattering paperwork. Without stopping to think, or even look, she pushed herself back off the floor and rolled, rather awkwardly, as the second drawer hit the ground inches from her, cracking the concrete floor with the force of its impact.

Looking up from where she was still sprawled on the ground, she could see the third drawer rocketing towards her, too fast and too close for her to avoid this time. Tensing her whole body, she raised her hands across her face in a hopeless attempt to shield herself and was extremely surprised when nothing happened. Peeking through the gaps in her fingers she could see the last metal drawer hanging motionless in the air a few metres away. As she lowered her hands, the reason for this became clear. The drawer was wrapped in familiar dark tendrils, which once again ran from her wrists, hanging between her and the drawer like dark, oily streamers.

"Impressive." Isenbard hadn't moved from his spot in the centre of the room. He was stood looking at Nora with a slightly quizzical expression. He didn't look scared, just vaguely interested, like a dog trainer who had just seen their pet do an unexpected trick. "I had heard that you had developed some interesting... abilities within Reverie, but to see them used back here too, and all on your own... well that is a treat."

Thinking of the voice that had warned her earlier, and which even now kept nudging her to chuck the filing cabinet drawer back at Isenbard, Nora wasn't completely sure that she was actually all on her own, but decided to keep that nugget of information to herself.

"Of course," Isenbard continued. "It's not like you're the only one who can do unusual things." He raised both hands and the machinery to either side of him rumbled increasingly loudly, shaking violently until the panels holding them together gave way. This left the guts of the machines hanging in the air, cables and bolts, screws and circuit boards all floating a metre or so off the ground. Even at this distance, Nora decided that most of the pieces looked much pointier, sharper or otherwise nastier than she was comfortable with.

"After my unfortunate mishap the last time we met, when your young friend managed to ruin my beautiful Horror, my Queen decided I needed something of an 'upgrade'." Isenbard shuddered for a moment, his casual, mocking tone replaced with something rawer and more primal. He held up his right hand, holding a small, dark stone between thumb and forefinger.

"A while ago we found a rich seam of these stones," he told Nora, turning the stone slowly as he spoke. Rather than catching the light as you might expect, the stone seemed to be in permanent shadow, as if it was sucking any available light into itself. "Compressed memories of nightmares, which give me even more power than I had before."

"So now you run on batteries," Nora snapped back, thinking of Adam's description of the mines he and the others had escaped from and the strange rocks that the Nightmares had been so keenly searching for.

"I suppose so," Isenbard replied, not in the least perturbed, "each one of these contains a lot of power... and I am full to the brim." He squeezed the stone tightly in his fist as he spoke, and wisps of dark, acrid smoke drifted out from between his fingers. When he opened his hand the stone was gone, all that remained were a few specks of ash-like dust, which he blew nonchalantly from his open palm.

When he turned his attention back to Nora his eyes were wide, fizzing with the sudden influx of power. "Ready or not..." he said with an unpleasant grin, "here I come..."

A whispered warning at the back of Nora's brain made her throw herself flat to the ground, and a split-second later another of the filing cabinet drawers rocketed through the air, missing her by inches. She realised that Isenbard had been trying to distract her, keeping her talking while he had lined up another of the metal drawers to hurl at her... and that it had very nearly worked.

Scowling with disappointment, Isenbard raised both his hands above his head, and several of the pieces of machinery that were still hovering menacingly behind Isenbard rose higher into the air in response to his command.

Knowing what was coming next, Nora looked around desperately and reflexively reached out towards the struts either side of a small gap in one of the larger machines a few metres away. Although it was still well out of her reach, the black tendrils that hung from her wrists seemed to understand exactly what she needed and shot across the room, wrapping themselves around the struts. Then, without a pause, Nora was sling-shot under the table like a pebble being fired from a catapult, just as the shards of metal that had been gathering above her crashed into the ground, obliterating the spot she had just left.

She skidded awkwardly to a stop on the other side of the factory, bruised by her slide across the concrete floor, and pushed herself into a standing position, trying to spot Isenbard.

"I see you..." came his mocking voice from somewhere far across the room, and there was a high-pitched buzzing noise as a swarm of smaller chunks of metal raced across the room towards her.

Once again the black tendrils saved her, this time flicking another, smaller table up in front of her as a shield, which shook violently with the impact of the flying shards as they hit it, several passing part-way through the table top before quivering to a halt.

Nora realised that she was fighting what would ultimately be a losing battle. So far she had been lucky and managed to avoid whatever Isenbard had thrown (quite literally) at her, but it was only a matter of time before one of his missiles managed to get through. Unsure whether it was a good idea or a really, really bad one, she concentrated on the nearest set of lights and one of the dark tentacles whipped out and shattered the bulb with a sharp cracking noise.

"What are you doing, little girl?" Isenbard shouted from across the room. "Don't you remember what it was like to exist within the Horror I created, shut away, all alone in the dark."

Nora knew that his words were intended to distract her, to hurt her, make her question herself. She knew enough of Isenbard by now to understand that was how he worked, chipping away at your fears and self-doubts. Despite this knowledge and her determination that she wouldn't let it work this time, she couldn't help but think back to the time she had spent trapped in the giant whirling Horror that Isenbard had created.

"Don't let him get in your head," she muttered to herself stubbornly, pushing the unpleasant memories that threatened to overwhelm her back into the far recesses of her mind. As she did, she flicked out two more of the tendrils, shattering two more of the nearest lights and dropping the corner of the factory into darkness.

"I'll still find you." Isenbard's mocking voice echoed off the walls. "You're just delaying the inevitable."

Nora's eyes darted left and right as she tried to work out what to do next. She knew, deep down, that Isenbard was right. It was only a matter of time until he found her. Off to her left, she could still see the outline of the entrance to the storage area she had spotted earlier, which looked like the only part of the building she hadn't yet investigated. She took a tentative step towards the doorway and then froze as a tall silhouette stepped out, directly between her and the door.

Isenbard didn't seem to have seen her yet. Instead, he turned his head from side to side, nose lifted skywards as if he was sniffing the air.

Looking desperately around Nora tried to spot another way to get around him, but there was no obvious option. She was surrounded by a graveyard of old machinery on two sides, Isenbard blocking her route on the third. Directly behind her was the external wall to the building, heavy metal shutters sealing the large windows tightly, with only the smallest chink of sunlight sneaking through.

The speck of light gave Nora the beginning of an idea. It was one that seemed both extremely risky and highly likely to go wrong, but her adventures with Adam had taught her that foolhardy plans sometimes did work out, otherwise Adam wouldn't ever have achieved anything.

Thinking about Adam, remembering their adventures together, and most oddly, a particularly clear memory of his shyly embarrassed smile when they had spoken about Reverie for the first time, filled her with a new determination. He was trapped somewhere in the land of the Nightmares and had trusted her to finish what he had started. Trusted her to find his mum and save her before it was too late.

She clenched her fist, gathering her courage.

"Hey... I'm over here!" she yelled at Isenbard's shadowy outline. "Come and get me... if you can."

Isenbard whipped around to face her, giving a short barking laugh. "Admirable bravery," he drawled, "pointless and empty, but admirable none the less."

Several long strides and he was within a few metres of Nora, where he stood staring at her, head cocked to one side and arms crossed.

"So now what?" He asked her, eyebrow raised quizzically. "You have led me a merry enough dance, but it ends here and now."

Nora scowled back, eyes narrowing with barely suppressed anger. To her surprise, she didn't feel in the least afraid, despite everything that Isenbard had put her through and the bad memories he had tried to bring back to life. Rather she felt angry, keen to lash out and bring the whole building crashing down on the pair of them.

She knew she could do it. She could feel a new strength rushing through her veins, growing even more potent every time she whipped out one of the shadowy tentacles. But she also knew that she had to save Adam's mum, and collapsing the factory seemed unlikely to achieve that, so instead she drew a deep steadying breath and prepared herself.

As Isenbard took a step towards her, unfolding his arms and flexing his fingers, Nora flicked out one of the tendrils from her wrist, but rather than aiming it at Isenbard, she wrapped it around the metal sheeting covering the large window behind her.

With a tortured screech the cover was ripped clear, lifted high above her head, and a shaft of bright sunlight flooded through. Isenbard stumbled back, temporarily blinded by the sudden light, raising his hands to shield his eyes.

Taking advantage of the distraction, his guard dropping for the briefest of moments, Nora brought the metal window cover crashing down with every ounce of strength she possessed. Isenbard was knocked from his feet, the smug grin disappearing from his face, replaced with a look of disbelief and shock in the split second before he collapsed under the weight of Nora's attack.

Nora sank back against the wall behind her, sliding slowly down it as her legs gave way, shaking uncontrollably as a backlog of stored up adrenaline hit her in one giant wave.

One of Isenbard's arms was sticking out from under the pile of twisted metal heaped upon him, and as Nora stared at it, one the outstretched fingers twitched slightly.

Willing some strength back into her uncooperative limbs, Nora slowly pushed herself back into a standing position, then cautiously she worked her way around Isenbard's sprawled figure, trying to stay as far away from him as she could.

As she reached the door to the storage area, Isenbard's hand clenched, fingers clawing at the concrete of the floor.

Trying to stay calm, Nora pushed against the door and wasn't very surprised to find it firmly locked. Even as recently as a few minutes ago that might have bothered her, but now without pausing she reached out with one of her shadowy limbs and pulled the door cleanly from its hinges, tossing it across the room, where it ricocheted off the ceiling before crashing to the ground.

The room beyond the doorway was musty and grey in the half-light that spilled through from the main building. There, tucked away in the corner was a shape, swaddled in a mix of blankets and an old sleeping bag. On any other occasion, Nora would have assumed that it was some unfortunate soul living rough, using the storage room as a place to shelter from the elements, but she knew immediately that she had found who she had been looking for.

As she took a tentative step towards the huddled figure there was a crashing noise from somewhere behind her, the sound of sheets of metal being displaced and a roar of pain and anger.

Knowing that there was no time to waste, Nora knelt down and pulled away the top-most blanket covering the figure.

The face that was revealed was undoubtedly Adam's mother. The face was thin and gaunt, the skin greyer than it should be, but it was most definitely her. Whatever she had been through, and whatever her impossibly prolonged sleep had done to her, the wide mouth and the gentle smile lines around her eyes were unmistakable.

"I hope this works," Nora murmured, before leaning forward and lifting a thin arm from amongst the bundled blankets. There was a faint mark on the little finger of her hand, a band of paler skin, so it was there that Nora placed the ring that Adam had entrusted her with.

As she did there was a further crashing noise behind her, and then heavy, slightly uneven footsteps echoed through the storage room.

Nora rose to her feet, letting Adam's mother's hand drop limply to the ground as she turned to face Isenbard. His face was bruised, one eye swelled closed, but his smile remained. It was a little crooked and his lip was split, but it seemed that pretty much nothing was capable of denting Isenbard's confidence, not even being buried under a huge pile of sheet steel.

"So here we all are," he said, rolling his shoulders back with a wince as he spoke. "You, me, an old Daydreamer... and whatever strange Nightmare you have started carrying around with you."

Feelings of uncontrollable anger surged through Nora as she faced the man who had tried to use her as a tool to further his own crazy scheme to bring down the barrier between the two worlds.

As she prepared to whip out one of her tendrils, determined to wipe the smug grin from his face, Isenbard raised both his hands, one of the dark stones clutched in each. With a slight grimace, he squeezed both hands tightly closed, wisps of acrid smoke drifting between each clenched fist.

The effect was immediate, waves of power emanating from him, so strong that Nora was nearly knocked off her feet. When Isenbard looked back up at her, his eyes crackled with scarcely contained energy.

Nora tried lashing out at him, but the twisting coil of darkness she flicked in his direction fizzed and sparked when it touched him, seeming to cause him no discomfort, but sending a pulse of nausea back to her.

As he took a step towards her, she tried another attack, and again was rewarded with nothing but a wave of sickness when she made contact with him. This time it was so severe that she ended up doubled over, eyes watering, hardly able to maintain her footing.

"It ends here," Isenbard growled, seeming to find it hard to form the words, dark sparks crackling between his teeth as unnatural energy coursed through him. "You put up a good fight, but in the end..." Then he paused, eyes widening at something over Nora's shoulder.

"No," he snarled, "It can't be...", stumbling back as he spoke.

As he did, Nora felt a slim hand resting on her shoulder, and then the familiar voice of Adam's mother speaking gently just behind her.

"Thank-you Nora, thank-you for everything, but I can take it from here."

The hand gave her shoulder a reassuring squeeze and then brightness filled the room, spreading outwards in an expanding, blinding bloom of light, forcing Nora to shield her eyes. Between the gaps in her fingers, she could just about make out Isenbard's broad, powerful outline, his arms outstretched in front of him, wisps of darkness still streaming from his fists. Then the wave of light reached him, the shadowy figure wavered and then was gone, blinking out of existence as if he had never been there.

"What... how?" Nora managed, as the light faded away, leaving her standing in the gently smouldering ruins of an otherwise very ordinary factory.

She turned to face Adam's mother, who was still glowing gently. Then the light that had filled her faded, leaving her looking human once again, human and very, very tired.

"How did you do that. I thought that you had run here to hide from Isenbard, but you just..." Nora stopped again, too stunned by everything she had been through to say any more.

However, it seemed that Adam's mum understood, managing to crease her exhausted features into something close to a relieved smile. "I did," she admitted. "I was afraid of him, I knew what he was capable of, what he could... and would do." Then she shrugged. "But I have spent the last few weeks living amongst the Nightmares, stuck in the middle of their world... and I didn't waste that time. I learned... I learned a lot."

Her expression darkened again. "Besides which... they have my boy..."

She stared down at the cheap, tacky ring now sat firmly on her little finger. "I've missed this. Thank you again for returning it to me. I know how much you risked, and for someone you didn't even really know."

At this, Nora looked down, slightly embarrassed. "I didn't just do it for you," she admitted, "although I am glad that you're okay. I did it for Adam, it's the last thing he asked me to do... the last thing before..." She stopped, the memory of Adam disappearing into the shadows stunting her words.

"I know," Adam's mother replied, clenching her fist tightly, a pale but growing light emanating from the ring now sat firmly on her little finger. "And now, thanks to you we can find him... find him and bring him back safe. Now let's get back to Reverie."

CHAPTER 21

For the first time he could think of, Adam was desperately missing school. Right about now he was pretty sure he should be awake, back in the real world and about to sit his maths exam. Unfortunately for him, none of those things were happening. Instead, he was dangling uncomfortably by his arms, which were stretched out above his head and tied securely to a very solid hook embedded into a wooden frame overhead. He knew his arms were tied securely, as he had tried with no success whatsoever to wriggle his wrists loose for the last hour. All he had achieved were very sore, and now quite badly chaffed wrists. He knew that the hook was solid as he had tried lifting his legs and tugging with all his weight to see if he could pull the hook loose. This had also failed completely but had resulted in his shoulders getting their fair share of the pain that had been restricted to his arms until then.

He stopped his futile attempts at escape and stared once again at the small table, placed no more than five metres away from him, on which his pendant now took pride of place. It had been snatched from him pretty much as soon as he had appeared back in the centre of the Queen's throne room, spat out of the murky darkness of the nightmare portal like a chunk of discarded rubbish. He had seen Nora, Lucid and Grimble's final despairing exit, unable to call to them as several of the Nightmares had grabbed hold of him, one of them ripping the pendant from his neck while he was still groggy and disorientated. Then he was pretty sure he had heard a loud explosion and the angry cries of the Nightmares across the cavern, although he couldn't see anything through the mass of monsters that had been clustered all around him.

He had blacked out for a while after that. But without the pendant, rather than waking back in the Waking World as he normally would have, he lost himself in genuine unconsciousness. When he woke again it was to find himself in his present predicament, dangling uselessly like some awful, ungainly wind-chime.

He was pretty sure that his pendant had been placed on the table next to where he was hanging specifically to taunt him. Close enough to see, almost close enough to reach out and grab, but still completely and frustratingly out of his grasp. Beyond the table and its gently glimmering treasure was the Queen's throne, where Ephialtes still sat, twirling a strand of dark hair around a long, outstretched nail. Her other hand was resting protectively over the small music box, bony fingers running across the wooden lid almost continuously, as if she was constantly needing to remind herself it was real.

Adam gave the music box a particularly venomous glare. He knew that it was just a small, wooden box and therefore completely innocent of any crime, but after all he had been through, including nearly losing his mind and being eaten by a skyscraper-sized Nightmare, to see it there under Ephialtes' talons and to know he was responsible for putting it there, made him feel quite sick.

"Probably not the best plan in the world to trust the word of the famously evil and untrustworthy Queen of Nightmares," he thought bitterly. The only comfort he could find within his otherwise desolate situation was the thin hope that Nora and the others had managed to escape the pursuing Nightmares and get the ring back to his mother. Ephialtes had been furious about that, incandescent with rage, snarling and cursing Adam and his friends.

It was very obvious now that she had never intended to let Adam leave with the ring, using it like an irresistibly shiny lure on a fishing line to reel him in, so it had given him a certain amount of satisfaction that she had underestimated him and his friends. While he may not have escaped her clutches, the ring looked like it may have, and the more time that passed without Ephialtes appearing to get any further news, the stronger his hope that Nora had managed to escape became.

Lost in his thoughts for the moment, Adam didn't immediately notice Ephialtes rising to her feet and stepping down from the throne, her long dress trailing along the ground behind her. She did, however, get his full attention when she walked across to the small table and placed down her music box, lifting his pendant in its place, wrapping the cheap chain around her fingers and letting it dangle it in front of her face.

"Strange isn't it," she told him, watching the gentle swing of the pendant like a cat, "strange the things we choose. The things that give us power, that make us different." She sighed, rather theatrically. "But you didn't pick this little trinket, did you, Daydreamer. I think this trinket chose you." Her eyes narrowed as she continued to stare at it.

"And I think I know why and how this little pendant came to be. Your mother wasn't the only thorn in my side. There was another who I found particularly troublesome, a rogue dream being who was audacious enough to give himself a name... Hugo. Then one day struggling with injuries that would have finished a lesser being, he vanished completely without a trace, disappeared along with your mother, never to be seen again... or so we thought. When you destroyed Isenbard's Horror he told me that you carried an odd pendant, one that gave you power, and he shared his suspicions about it with me."

Ephialtes paused and moved a little nearer to Adam, holding the pendant closer to his face, making sure he could clearly see it.

"That crazy theory of Isenbard's ate away at me," she continued. "At first, I dismissed it as the ravings of a man who had seen all his

197

careful scheming come to nothing, a sign of his empty frustration. But the more I thought about it and the more I heard about this... boy who could control dreams far beyond anything someone his age should ever be able to manage, the more I began to believe that perhaps... he was right."

She thrust her face even closer to Adam, looking straight into his eyes with her own flat, empty pupils.

"I think you have suspected the same thing yourself for a while now, haven't you Daydreamer? That this pendant is more than your link to this world, more even than the key to unlocking your Daydreams."

She scooped up the pendant onto the palm of one hand and lifted the other above it, one long, sharp nail pointing directly downwards. "Strange little thing isn't it. The way it glows and pulses, almost as if it has a life of its own."

As she finished speaking, she thrust down her nail, pressing it hard against the pendant. Her mouth twisted into a cruel smile as she exerted pressure, a small wisp of smoke spiralling up from the pendant, which had started to glow gently.

"Stop it!" Adam shouted, any thoughts of his own wellbeing completely forgotten. He tried to throw himself forward but only succeeded in jarring his arms uncomfortably. "Stop... leave it alone!"

"I am afraid not," Ephialtes replied, as she continued to squeeze. "You, your mother... and your father have all got in my way time and time again. You may have managed to steal your mother's ring away from me, but with the destruction of this shabby little trinket I will be rid of your Daydreaming and, if Isenbard's theory is correct, all that is left of your troublesome father at the same time."

Adam tried not let the horror he felt show in his face, although deep down he knew that she was right and the panic he now felt as he watched her pressing down on the pendant was threatening to completely consume him. He had suspected, ever since he had found the portrait of his mother standing with Hugo in the Mansion back in Nocturne, that the pendant held greater secrets than he had first thought. Time and time again the pendant had saved him when he needed help, and Adam could still clearly recall the voice that had occasionally seemed to come from within it, advising him, helping him. He didn't know what remnant of Hugo lived on within the pendant, but he was convinced that some part of his father was still in there, watching over him and keeping him safe.

It didn't seem fair. He had come so far to find his mum and had come within touching distance of saving her. It was that thought that had kept him going no matter how difficult everything had become, when things had been too much to cope with, when he had been exhausted and beaten down. He had known that when the time came his mum would be able to explain about Hugo and the pendant, and that in a strange way they would be together as a family... just a slightly unusual one. But now he had no idea if his mum was safe... and the pendant was being destroyed in front of his eyes. Everything that he had fought so hard for was being ripped away and he felt powerless to stop it.

Trying to calm himself, to stop his mind sinking into uncontrollable despair, Adam concentrated as hard as he could. He knew that his mother had managed to Daydream without her ring, so surely he could do the same without his pendant. It was just he had never managed it before, always having the pendant to fall back on, sometimes managing to summon Daydreams without really knowing what he was doing.

He glared at Ephialtes bitterly, gritting his teeth and refusing to let out the tears he could feel welling up. He tried to summon the feeling he got whenever he Daydreamed, but without the comforting glow of the pendant, it felt impossible. Closing his eyes tightly he started digging back through his memories, trying to find something that would help, even the smallest and simplest of dreams, just enough to release his arms and give him the chance to stop Ephialtes, no matter how slim that chance might be.

He was concentrating so hard that when his arms were suddenly released it caught him completely by surprise and he dropped to the ground awkwardly.

"I did it... I managed a Daydream without needing the pendant," was the second thought that went through Adam's mind as he hit the rocky floor, the first thought being, "Ouch!". But when he opened his eyes, he realised that it was something entirely different that had released him.

In the few seconds since he had closed his eyes the Throne room had descended into chaos. From his prone position on the floor, he could see Nora off to one side, dark tentacles whirling around her head like a bullwhip. Seeing him looking across she gave him a fierce grin and lifted her thumb in greeting, before bringing one of the tendrils whirling past his face, straight at Ephialtes, who batted it to one side with a snarl.

Rolling to one side and pushing himself awkwardly onto his feet, Adam looked across to his other side and was greeted with the sight of a figure that was instantly recognisable and yet completely unfamiliar at the same time.

"Mum?"

The figure ignored him, concentrating fully on Ephilates instead. It looked like his mum, the same short stature and determined expression that he had so desperately missed, but he certainly wasn't used to seeing his mum glowing, light flickering all around her like the flame around a candle-wick.

His mother raised her hand and the glimmering light that surrounded her focused around the ring that was now sat on her little finger. Even with all the craziness going on around him, and despite the pain in his arms (and the ache that was now pretty much everywhere else in his body) Adam felt a warm glow of achievement.

Ephialtes was shouting something, but Adam couldn't make it out over the background noise all around him. There were roars, hisses, and grunts from the mass of Nightmares still in the cavern, and from across the throne room a series of loud explosions that sent shockwaves of sound through the air, nearly knocking Adam back off his feet.

His mum had her eyes squeezed closed in concentration and moments later a flurry of small particles of light shot out from the fingers of her raised hand, heading directly towards Ephialtes. In response Ephialtes raised her own arms, her long hair floating around her like she was submerged underwater.

The lank strands of hair moved with a life of their own, shielding Ephialtes from the shards of light, which ricocheted across the cave, splintering the stone of the walls and ceiling and raining splinters of rock down on them all. One final particle of light, even brighter than the others, made it past Ephialtes' defences and struck her raised hand. She shrieked in anger, and as she recoiled reflexively, Adam saw his pendant fly clear of her grip and loop through the air.

Without stopping to think Adam dived forwards, arms outstretched, reaching for the small, glinting shape. Everything seemed to slow around him as his fingers brushed the edge of the pendant. He felt like he was frozen in time, and every detail of the battle now raging across the cavern suddenly became clear.

To one side Nora was still standing, holding off a dozen or more of the Nightmares. She had picked up one of the largest monsters with one of her long, dark tendrils and was currently swinging it around like a ragdoll, apparently using it to hit the others. To the other side his mother was still caught up in a fierce exchange with Ephialtes, currently throwing up a shield of light around herself as the Nightmare Queen struck back at her, impossibly long strands of her hair snapping out towards his mother like Medusa's snakes.

Further across the cavern, Adam could see the mismatched pairing of Lucid and Grimble in the middle of their own impossible looking clash with another large group of Nightmares. Grimble was roaring insults and throwing out all sorts of random potions and inventions which fizzed and sparked all around him, making him look for all the world like an angry and very hairy Catherine Wheel, while alongside him Lucid span a pair of long sticks with surprising dexterity. Adam could remember how useless Lucid had felt during their very first battle with the Nightmares and knew that he had been practicing intently, night after night. From the look of it, all that training had paid off, Lucid's awkward, lanky form now moving with surprising grace. His long limbs were swinging the sticks with enough momentum to knock even the larger Nightmares from their feet.

Things appeared to have been further confused by the arrival of another, much smaller group of Nightmares with the unmistakable figure of Mittens at their forefront. They had crashed into the room like a battering ram, scattering the Queen's followers to either side and making their way rapidly towards Adam.

Then the pendant was within his grasp, his fingers tightened around it, and time returned to normal. He hit the ground with a bump, leaving him winded, but he was on his feet again in seconds, reaching out in his mind for a Daydream. He didn't have the time to be creative and settled on the first one that came to mind. He remembered a dream where he had been lost in space, where he floated freely in a world without gravity, but this time rather than it having an effect upon him, he imagined a world where it affected everyone else. Focusing his attention on the nearest group of Nightmares he lifted both his hands and saw their aggressive grimaces turn to almost comical confusion as they were lifted gently up from the ground, floating towards the ceiling of the cavern.

For a minute it looked like they might make it, the various groups all working their way towards the spot where Adam was stood, the element of surprise making up for the huge imbalance in numbers. Then, slowly but surely, the sheer mass of Nightmares, no matter how confused and disorganised, began to slow his friends progress.

Adam redoubled his efforts, but he could only affect a relatively small number of Nightmares at any one time. He could already feel sweat breaking out on his brow and his breathing was becoming more laboured, each inward breath stinging his lungs. Looking around he could see his friends were also struggling. To one side Mittens and the rest of her rag-tag freedom fighters were now surrounded, their route to Adam completely blocked, with no prospect of retreat or escape. To his other side, Nora was still battling gamely, now using two unfortunate Nightmares to swat away the others that pressed in all around her, but it was clear she couldn't maintain the level of energy it needed to keep the Nightmares off her for much longer. Off in the distance, he thought he could still see Lucid's top hat bobbing above the crowds, then there was a faint cry as it vanished from sight.

Closest to him, his mother was still locked in her struggle with Ephialtes, white flashes of light matching the flying strands of the Queen's dark hair in an exchange of blows so fast Adam's eyes watered just trying to keep track of their movements. Even in this clash, it seemed as if his mother's earlier efforts had drained her, every now and then one of the Queens stabbing attacks would slip through his mother's defences, leaving sickly looking marks wherever they struck her skin.

Adam could feel himself starting to tire as well. He had been through a lot in the last few busy, horrendous hours, all of which had taken its toll. But even taking all of that into account he was still finding his Daydreaming harder than he knew it should be. There was something about the Queen's cavern that was sucking away his energy, somehow limiting what he was able to do. His mind flashed back to the mine and the dark rocks that the Nightmares had been so keen to find, tiny stones which sucked away the light and gave the Nightmares even greater strength. As this memory swam in front of his eyes, he took another chance to look around the cavern, and it was then that he saw them. All around the Queen's cavern were tall, slender structures, which he had originally mistaken as candlesticks. But looking more closely he could see that, rather than a candle, each one was topped with one of the small dark stones. As he lifted the nearest group of Nightmares into the air, the black rock pulsed and he could see the shadows gathering in the air around it, as it reacted to his Daydreaming.

It might have been his imagination, but it felt like the air was thickening slightly around him, his last couple of breaths even more difficult than the last. Next to him, his mother had dropped to her knees, still fending off the Queen's attacks but fading fast, and to his other side, Nora was close to being completely enveloped.

Trying to summon every last bit of energy that he had, Adam braced himself to attempt one giant, final Daydream, but before he could finish the room was shaken by one further surprise arrival. Through increasingly blurry eyes Adam saw the completely improbable sight of the circus troupe careering madly across the cavern, Oomba was leading the way, his crash helmet wedged so tightly onto his head that it seemed unlikely he could see anything at all. This didn't seem to be stopping him though, instead, it meant that as he charged across the room, he was inflicting a series of very painful looking headbutts at a very unfortunate height. Behind him, Aggro was bellowing and looking more like an angry Rhino than ever, while the tall figure of Augustus the Ringmaster strode alongside him. Meanwhile the twin acrobats Pixie and Trixie flipped across the room, too slight to do much damage to the Nightmares, but too nimble to be caught, leading several of the clumsier Nightmares to accidentally hit themselves in the face or clobber their nearest neighbour as they tried unsuccessfully to grab hold of the darting figures.

And there, right in the middle of them all, was the unmistakable figure of Bella, her clockwork arm making short work of any Nightmare unfortunate enough to get too close. It seemed that the circus troupe were doing what they could to clear a path for her, and although it seemed unlikely that they could keep it up for long, it was working. The Nightmare's attention had been split between the various groups of Adam's friends and it had left a route to Adam which was comparatively unguarded.

Within a few seconds Bella was alongside him grabbing him roughly by the arm. "You look like you could use some help Daydreamer," she told him with a twisted smile. "I should probably have taken my payment and set sail after I got the Mayfly shipshape again... but where would the fun have been in that! So instead I came looking for you... and bumped into that unruly lot again." She pointed to the circus troupe, who had formed a loose protective ring around the two of them. "So, what's the matter with you? I thought you could just... you know..." she raised her fingers and waggled them in a vaguely mystical way.

"I tried, but the Nightmares have got these weird stones that are making it really hard for me to do anything," Adam admitted. "If only I was nearer to the Weave... or the sea of dreams, maybe then I would be strong enough." His shoulders slumped and the nearest group of Nightmares that had been bobbing around the ceiling of the cavern came crashing down, as he let his concentration slip.

"Hmmm," Bella looked at him, her expression thoughtful. "I remember what happened out on the Dwam when you tried to use your power, seems like it filled you right up, so much you could hardly contain it."

Seeming to come to a decision within herself, she tipped back her head and reached up with the fingers of her good hand. There was a brief, rather unpleasant noise, and when she faced Adam again there was an empty socket where the glow of her newly acquired eye had been. Reaching out nonchalantly with her other arm, the clockwork joints ticking gently to themselves, she knocked a Nightmare who had managed to get past the circus troupe from its feet, then she held out her hand, lit by the glow of the gem, bright in the surrounding darkness.

"I think this is why the Deep Sleeper really let you take one of her gems," she said, unable to completely hide the tinge of loss in her voice. "The power of thousands of years of dreams, crystalised in your hand, right here, right now, exactly when and where you need it the most."

Adam looked at her dumbfounded for a moment, aware of how much she was giving up. Then he nodded sharply, squared his shoulders and lifted the shining gem above his head.

He hadn't got the vaguest idea what he needed to do next, or how best to use the power that Bella had handed him, but if nothing else he had managed to attract the attention of the whole cavern, the glow of the gem increasingly bright. There was a rumbling echo across the cavern, an ancient sound that reminded him of the mournful cry of the Deep Sleeper, then with a resounding cracking noise, the nearest of the dark stones that were scattered across the cavern shattered.

"Nooooo!" Ephialtes cried out. "What are you doing. How... how are you..." but her cries were drowned out by a series of further loud explosions as, one after another, the black rocks blew apart. With the destruction of each stone Adam could feel himself getting stronger, the previous heavy, oppressive sensation that had held him back lifting. Looking around he could see that his companions were also benefiting from the sudden change. His mother had regained her feet and the glow that had surrounded her had intensified to the degree that Adam had to squint just to look in her direction. To his other side Nora gave a victorious whoop, while at the far end of the chamber he could see that Mittens and her unlikely squad of freedom fighters had broken through their attackers and reached Lucid and Grimble, who, despite looking battered and bruised, had both managed to regain their feet.

By now the brightness of the gem was so strong that Adam daren't look at it, using all his concentration just to keep it raised above his head. There was another great, ancient rumbling echo which shook the cavern, knocking many of the remaining Nightmares from their feet. But rather than making Adam afraid, the sound filled him with a sense of complete peace. Then he closed his eyes and remembered a perfect dream.

Behind him a whirling circle of pure white light appeared, initially small but growing rapidly until it was five, then ten metres across. The Nightmare nearest to it turned its head to one side, confused by its sudden appearance, then howled as it was sucked into the glowing portal. One after another the other Nightmares spread across the cavern followed suit. Some hung grimly onto the nearest rocky outcrops, but the force dragging them in was so strong that the rocks themselves were pulled from the ground, following the unfortunate Nightmares through the spinning circle of light. Within a few, chaotic moments, the cavern was almost completely empty, only Adam's companions and Ephialtes remaining.

She was still standing, several of the dark wisps of her hair coiling in the air around her while she used the rest to tether herself to the ground, resisting the drag of the portal behind Adam.

"What have you done?" she gasped, looking over Adam's shoulder. "Where have you sent them."

"I remembered a perfect dream," Adam replied, "...and the place where all the perfect dreams happen."

The brightness behind him faded a little and the detail of the scene within the whirling light became clearer. There were trees and plants stretching out as far as the eye could see, and off in the distance a large, placid shallow lake with a great cave at its centre. It was exactly as he remembered the Garden, before he had seen its true nature.

"No... I can't go there. I won't..." Ephialtes skin had somehow turned even paler, and for the first time Adam felt she looked truly afraid. One by one the strands of hair that gripped the floor and the sides of the cavern were pulling loose, and as they did her feet rose from the ground, leaving her hanging horizontally in the air as she continued to fight the pull of the Garden.

"Fine," she snarled, staring at Adam with a look of pure hatred, "but if I go there, it won't be alone." One, long grasping strand of her hair whipped out and wrapped itself around Adam's mother, then there was a splintering sound as the last of the hair anchoring Ephialtes to the ground gave way and she shot across the room towards the portal, Adam's mum dragged along behind her.

Things had happened so fast that no one had been able to react quickly enough to stop her. Too late Nora reached out with her shadowy tentacles, but they flailed against empty air, missing Adam's mum by centimetres.

Adam tried to find a Daydream, but there wasn't enough time. Then a glint just across from him caught his eye, the edge of Ephialtes' music box reflecting the spreading light from the spot where it had fallen to the floor.

Reaching out, Adam grabbed the music box, and shouting loudly to attract Ephialtes attention, threw it in a high, looping arc. Even as she was being dragged through the air Adam could see her looking up, her empty, flat eyes locking hungrily onto the sight of the small box spinning through the air. For an infinitely long split-second he could see her face torn with indecision, then with a shudder she released Adam's mum, who dropped to the floor, bouncing awkwardly before rolling to a stop just clear of the whirling portal. The long, lank, strand of dark hair that had been holding her flicked across the cavern, grabbing hold of the music box as it dropped back towards the ground and pulling it protectively into Ephialtes grasp. The last sight that Adam had of Ephialtes was of her cradling the music box tightly, her face looking momentarily younger, perhaps even happy. Then she was gone, the portal vanishing behind her.

Adam dropped to his knees as the last of the energy in the gem fizzled away. With seconds he had gone from feeling indestructible to hardly being able to keep his head upright.

A few months before his adventures in Reverie had begun, Adam had suffered a horrible bout of the flu and found himself unable to get out of bed. When he had finally been able to get up it had been impossibly hard to do anything, other than stagger around in a haze. The feeling he had now was worse, but he didn't care. All around the cavern his friends... his family were scattered but safe, blinking as the light in the room returned to normal.

CHAPTER 22

A week had passed since the battle in the Queen's Cavern and a lot had happened in that time.

Isabella had managed to find space on her ship for the circus troupe and a handful of the other miners that had been previously been held prisoner by the Nightmares, along with Lucid and Grimble, who Adam had promised to visit back in Nocturne, just as soon as they reached the other side of their crossing of the Dwam. He had decided that his one voyage on the sea of dreams had probably been quite eventful enough and didn't need repeating, or at least not for a while.

"We will return when we get back to our vessel and collect more of the prisoners," Augustus had promised. "Without the Queen I am hopeful that the Nightmares will take some time to reorganise themselves, giving us a chance to free the rest. Our ship is large enough to carry them back to Nocturne and then perhaps... perhaps we can find something else to do with our time, seeing as piracy hasn't really worked out all that well."

Mittens and her crew of freedom fighters had also left shortly after the conclusion of the battle. Although only after one of them had enthusiastically daubed the symbol of the Triple F across one of the walls of the throne room. "This could be the start of a real change," Mittens had told Adam with satisfaction, "a sign that the tide has turned." Then she had led her group away down one of the tunnels, pausing briefly to mutter something to Nora, before yelling back, "I am sure I will see you around Daydreamer."

Adam asked Nora what it was that Mittens had said, but she had only smiled enigmatically at his question before muttering something about them arranging for a 'girl's night out'. Deciding that he would never understand girls, especially ones with super-powers and mysterious Nightmare friends, Adam hadn't pursued it any further and settled for just being glad that Nora was back, and his friend, once again.

That had just left him and his mother, who had turned to him straight after the battle with tired, but incredibly proud eyes, and said the three words that Adam had feared he would never hear again. "Let's go home."

It had initially felt odd to go back to his old room, odd but incredibly nice at the same time. Charlie's parents had been sad to see him leave, and Adam knew that he would never be able to properly repay them for the huge amount of generosity and kindness that they had shown him, but this didn't alter the overwhelming happiness he had felt when he and his mum had first opened the door back into their own house. He wasn't sure if Charlie's parents, or anyone else, were really convinced by the story of his mum's prolonged attack of amnesia, which had been used to explain both her mysterious and sudden disappearance and her inability to account for anything that had happened since, but that was a problem for the future. For now, all that mattered was going home and being their own small but perfectly formed family again.

Before he had said his goodnights and headed up to his room to go to bed, Adam and his mum had spent the evening watching a movie together, sitting in comfortably silent companionship side by side on their new sofa. It was a pretty horrible shade of lime green, and the pattern was similarly awful, but it had been cheap, which in the circumstances was about the best they could hope for. The sofa, a second-hand television, and a couple of replacement doors had been the first stage of the hurried repair and redecoration that they had enthusiastically thrown themselves into, erasing the signs of the Nightmare attack on their home which had started everything just a few months before.

There had been a lot to talk about after they had first returned together from Reverie, although some topics of conversation still hadn't been completely covered to Adam's satisfaction. Whenever he had raised a question about the pendant or about Hugo, his father, his mum had steered the conversation off in another direction, promising to answer Adam's questions in time.

Adam hadn't pushed his mum for answers so far, despite his burning need to know more, as he could tell this was a subject that his mum still found difficult, perhaps even painful, to talk about. So tonight Adam had decided to give his mum a break from the constant questions and instead they had enjoyed an evening of relative normality, just relaxing watching a repeat of an old comedy that they must have seen at least three times before, but which still made them both laugh.

It had been nice to do something so utterly normal, the familiarity of the film bringing back memories of the previous times that they had watched it together, when their biggest concern had been running out of popcorn or being interrupted by telesales calls just as the film got to the finale, but eventually the credits had rolled and Adam had made his way up to bed.

"Sweet dreams," his mum had shouted up to him as he made his way up the stairs, a new nightly ritual that she seemed to find funnier than Adam thought was necessary.

Then he had remembered that today (or tonight, depending on how you looked at it), was when he had arranged to meet up with Lucid and Grimble back in Nocturne, and he had bounced up the second half of the stairs with a broad grin on his face, keen to see how his friends were getting on now they had been back home for a couple of days.

CHAPTER 23

As it turned out Adam re-entered Reverie just in time to catch his two companions as they were about to start their breakfast, which he decided was particularly excellent timing.

"Morning Adam," Lucid greeted him, "come and join us, there is plenty."

Not needing much encouragement, with the spread of warm pieces of bread, butter and jams all looking very tempting, Adam pulled up a seat and joined his friends.

"So, what's been going on?" Adam asked, sensing an underlying buzz of excitement in the room.

"It's very strange," Grimble told him with scarcely contained merriment. "Apparently last night someone did something very, very foolish,"

"Or brave?" Lucid added.

"No... definitely foolish, although apparently also very lucky. This someone managed to break into Granny's offices and took every single memento, keepsake and other stolen treasure that she had been keeping as a reminder of the leverage she held over people."

Adam's thought back to the few minutes he had spent meeting Granny in the huge room, stuffed wall to wall with treasures teetering precariously on every available surface.

Lucid was also trying, rather unsuccessfully, to contain a grin by this point. "That must have come as a bit of a blow to her."

"Oh, it did," Grimble told him. "Apparently, after she found out, you could hear her shrieking all the way to the far end of the docks. Without her collection it seems that she can't remember exactly who still owes her a favour and even if she could, she can no longer prove it."

"But isn't it dangerous to cross someone like Granny?" Adam asked.

"Probably", Lucid shrugged. "I suppose whoever did it thought it worth the risk."

"And was it?" Adam asked pointedly, "was it worth the risk?"

"Sorry, no idea what you are talking about," Lucid said, refusing to meet Adam's gaze. Then looking across Adam's shoulder at the clock he muttered a quick curse under his breath. "Looks like I'm running a bit late... we can pick this up again later... not that there is anything to discuss of course... as I know nothing about it."

Stopping briefly to grab his long coat from the back of his chair and give Adam and Grimble a quick wave goodbye he made his way out of the room, leaving his friends to finish breakfast without him.

"Where is he off to so early," Adam said, "I have never known Lucid deliberately walk away from an unfinished meal."

"I think he has other and even more important unfinished business to attend to," Grimble told him, leaning back on his seat with a look close to satisfaction on his grizzled face. "He is off to meet Tremello. Apparently, she is part of a trading party that arrived at the docks late last night."

Lucid's nervous energy made more sense to Adam now, and he returned Grimble's contented smile with one of his own. "I'm glad," he said, "I think that he deserves a bit of happiness after all he has been through."

"I think we all do," Grimble grunted back. "Let's make a deal. For the next couple of weeks why don't we spend our time relaxing, eating, drinking, sleeping and not having to save the world even once... what do you say?"

"It's a deal," Adam told him, reaching out a hand which Grimble grasped and shook firmly.

"While you are here I wanted to show you this as well," Grimble added, gesturing back over his shoulder with one blunt thumb. An easel was resting against the wall, with a part- completed portrait illuminated by the first rays of sunlight bleeding through the Mansion's tall windows.

Although much of the detail was still missing, Adam could recognise the figures easily enough. There to one side was the tall, angular frame of Lucid, one hand resting companionably on the shoulder of the shorter, dour figure of Grimble. To the other was the sketch outline of a small girl, perfectly normal looking other than the long, dark tentacle whipping around above her head. In the background, there was a tall woman, wearing a long trenchcoat, the detail of one brass arm already picked out. Last of all, right in the centre of the portrait the first few lines of the fifth and final figure had been drawn in. A small boy, with dark unruly hair and a gentle glow centred around a pendant hanging from his neck.

"What do you think?" Grimble asked him, a friendly twinkle in his eyes. "It has been a while coming, what with the distractions of stopping the end of the world more than once in the last few weeks, but it seemed about time we decided on the new membership of the Five."

"I... I don't know if I..." Then Adam stopped himself, Grimble was right, they had prevented the end of the world, or at least postponed it, more than once... and he had been a big part of it. Whether he liked it or not, he was a Daydreamer and that had brought associated responsibilities.

"You know what... I like it," Adam said. "What do the others think?"

"Nora was all for it," Grimble said with a grin, "it will be the first time that a Nightmare, or at least part Nightmare has been a part of the Five... but I guess we all have to move with the times. As for Bella... we haven't quite had the chance to check with her yet. Still, that is something for another day."

Sitting back down and pouring himself a big mug of scaldingly hot tea, Adam settled back into his seat and let a feeling of long overdue contentment wash over him. For the moment the world was safe, and he had done his part to make it stay that way. Maybe tomorrow, or the next day, or next week some other calamity would appear on the horizon and he would find himself somehow caught in the middle of it all once again, but for now there was just companionship, food and well-deserved rest.

Across the city, at the edge of the docks, two tall figures strolled hand in hand along the waterfront, deep in conversation, long fingers tentatively entwined. Their words had been awkward at first, stilted and weighed down with too many years of separation, but surprisingly quickly the baggage of the past had been left behind and now they walked lightly and unencumbered.

Much further away, far across the ocean, a group of hideous looking nightmare monsters were sat around a large and horribly decorated table. Completely at odds with the rest of the group, but somehow also completely at home in their company, was a small girl, seated right at the head of the table. One at a time they raised a mismatched set of cup and mugs skywards in silent salute to absent comrades and in tribute to the victory that they had somehow managed to achieve.

Somewhere between the two groups, floating precariously on the surface of the great sea of dreams, a solitary figure stands proud and defiant on the deck of a ship, an insignificant but undeterred speck against the huge, raging majesty of the surrounding oceans. Storm clouds are gathering around her, but that only broadens her smile, the clouds a sign that her search is nearly at its end.

Finally, and infinitely high above the world, perched precariously at the top of a stairway that stretches ever onwards into the sky, there is a small room, and in the centre of that room a rickety bed. Looking closely the face of a small boy can be seen poking out from under the ruffled covers, peaceful and resting. His eyes are closed, deep in sleep, giving off a sensation of total peace and tranquillity.

And then, just for a moment, one eyelid flickers...

-THE END-

Printed in Great Britain
by Amazon